The Magic Violin
by Yvonne Venton

Text copyright © 2016 Yvonne Venton

All Rights Reserved

Book cover illustration by Tracy Sullivan

A story for all who love music..........

from 9 to 90

Table of Contents

Chapter 1

The Strange Violin Lesson

Chapter 2

The Concert

Chapter 3

The Adventure Begins

Chapter 4

Stradivarius' Workshop

Chapter 5

The Professor's Violin is Given Away

Chapter 6

The Soul of the Violin

Chapter 7

Nicolo Paganini

Chapter 8

Some Interesting Conversations

Chapter 9

The Market Place

Chapter 10

Dirty Dealings at the Auction

Chapter 11

Tarisio's Attic Home and his Remarkable 'Family'

Chapter 12

The Farm at Fontinato

Chapter 13

Margaret meets the 'Messiah' Strad.

Chapter 14

The Last Pieces of the Puzzle Fall into Place

Chapter 15

A Very Generous Lady

Chapter 16

An Unusual Violin Case

Chapter 17

Back Home

Chapter 1

The Strange Violin Lesson

The stars shone brightly and the frost glittered under the street lamp as Margaret opened the gate and walked up the path to the cottage where the Professor lived.

Eight o'clock was quite late for her to be out alone. Usually, her violin lesson was at four o'clock straight from school. But the Professor had been so busy lately that each week her lesson had been gradually getting later, until today, when he had sent a message asking if she could come at eight o'clock. Her mother didn't like her being out so late, even though she had just had her twelfth birthday, but Margaret was thrilled. After all, it was an honour to be a pupil of the Professor's. In fact, even if he had asked her to come at midnight, she wouldn't have thought twice about it.

She rang the bell and then turned to look up at the stars. There must be thousands of them, she thought. I wonder if there are worlds up there like ours, with trees and rivers, mountains and people. And then some people say if you wish upon a star, what you want most comes true. She closed her eyes and wished …… to pass her audition in April for the Menuhin School of Music. She'd dreamed of going there since she was seven years old and having her first lesson on a half size violin.

She was still gazing up when the door opened and the smiling face of Mrs Tucker the Professor's housekeeper, was framed in the doorway.

"Come in quickly Margaret. We mustn't let the cold air in."

Once inside, she took off her coat and scarf, then, picking up her violin case, she knocked softly at the door of the snug. She could never understand why her teacher insisted on calling the little room behind the kitchen, where he took his pupils, a 'snug'. It was certainly very cosy, with its soft carpet, powder blue curtains and grand piano which filled half the room, but 'snug' seemed such a funny word for a room,

"Come in."

The voice of the Professor came faintly through the thick door. Quietly, she opened it and her teacher looked up from some music he was studying and smiled. She took out her violin, carefully tuned it with the piano, and stood waiting for him to be ready.

"Carry on Margaret. I'm listening."

He usually listened while she played her last week's work right through. Then she would play it all again and he would stop her to point out the mistakes and sometimes show her exactly how each note should be played. Tonight, though, he seemed strangely unlike his normal self and was paying hardly any attention to her. In fact, she had finished playing the study twice before he said anything at all. Then, rather suddenly, as if he had only just realised she was there, he said,

"Good Margaret, yes ..... er ..... very good."

This was praise indeed. For he was hardly ever satisfied with her work.

"Shall I play the scales now?"

He nodded absently, and then Margaret got a second shock, for he handed her the book of scales.

Now everybody knows that scales have to be played from memory, and as a rule, the Professor was very strict about this. Puzzled, Margaret placed the book on her music stand, hesitated, then tightly closing her eyes, stared to play. She played each scale twice, then stopped.

"Yes. Good." He repeated in a faraway voice.

Somewhat mystified, and not being sure what do next, she said,

"Shall I play my new piece now Professor?"

He nodded. She played it and he nodded again. This was the most peculiar violin lesson she had ever had. No criticism, no correction, nothing but lukewarm praise. While she was thinking this, the Professor sprang the final surprise.

"No more. I think you've done enough for this evening Margaret. Put away your violin. I want to talk to you about tomorrow's concert."

Margaret stared at him in amazement. She'd only had twenty minutes. There was another twenty five to go …… and what concert? It was the first she had heard of it.

"A concert? Tomorrow night?"

The old man looked at her over the top of his glasses as if he was surprised to see her still standing there. Then, all of a sudden, he seemed to come down to earth.

"Oh, of course, of course. How foolish of me. I haven't told you about it yet. As you are my most promising pupil, I'm taking you to London tomorrow and to a concert in the evening."

"Really? How lovely. Is it something very special?"

Now this was a very silly question. He hardly ever went anywhere, so it must be very special to get him away from this comfortable cottage. His next words left her in no doubt.

"Yes indeed. I'm going to take you to hear the great Meltzac play, Margaret."

The dreamy look returned to his eyes, and a slow smile lit up his face. Iso Meltzac was one of the greatest of all living violinists, so you can imagine how thrilled she was. For a moment she was completely silent, then everything seemed to bubble up at once.

"Oh, how wonderful. I've heard lots of his recordings, but to see and hear the great Meltzac in person! I can hardly believe it. And ..... and he plays on a Stradivarius violin, doesn't he, Professor?" she finished breathlessly.

The old violin master got up from his chair, still with that faraway look in his eyes, and with a hint of sadness in his voice, answered very slowly,

"Yes, Margaret, Iso Meltzac plays on a Stradivarius violin."

Then he added after a long pause "My Stradivarius."

"Your Stradivarius?"

"Yes, my Stradivarius. It will always be mine you see, although I gave it to him many years ago. Did you know that the great Meltzac was once the pupil of your humble Professor? He is a genius, so in what better hands could my beloved violin be?"

Margaret just stared at him.

"You mean you had a real Stradivarius violin, and you gave it away?"

The Professor sighed and slowly nodded his head.

"It's a long story and I haven't time to tell you now, but when I was a young student the violin was given to me by a very kind lady, and ..... well, I'll tell you all about it one of these days."

Margaret looked at him wonderingly.

"If I had a Stradivarius violin, I don't think I could just give it away."

The Professor smiled at her.

"Oh yes you could Margaret. I'm quite sure you could."

Later that night, in bed, she thought about her music lesson, the strange mood of the old teacher, and the thrill of tomorrow's concert.

In her imagination she saw the huge concert hall packed with people. The orchestra tuning up. The sudden hush as the conductor mounted the rostrum and his funny little bobbing bows as he acknowledged the applause. Then the soloist would enter, and the clapping which had been dying away, would be redoubled in honour of the great violinist. In his hands he would hold the Stradivarius violin. Professor Mallais' violin. As she drifted off to sleep, she thought how wonderful it must be to hold such a wonderful instrument. A violin more than two hundred and fifty years old. A violin made by the very greatest of all violin makers. Old Stradivarius of Cremona. As she was imagining all this, she little thought that not only would she see and hear the great Meltzac, but she would actually hold it in her own two hands. With the strangest of consequences!

Chapter 2

The Concert

Margaret was up very early next morning, and right after breakfast she started to get ready for her trip to London. There wasn't really any need for her to be ready quite so soon, as the Professor wasn't calling for her until after lunch.

"For goodness sake Margaret." said her mother at last, as for the third time she turned round and bumped into her.

"Come and have some lunch ...... and take off your coat. You're not sitting down like that."

The village where they both lived didn't have a railway station of its own, so they had to get a bus to the nearby town of Haslemere and catch the train from there.

Professor Mallais arrive on time and after a twenty minute bus ride, they got out at the station with ten minutes to spare. The Professor went to the bookstall for a paper, but Margaret was much too excited to read. Soon they heard the signal clang down and a voice call out, "London train, London train. Calling at Witley, Milford, Godalming, Farncombe and Guildford and then fast to Waterloo. Hurry along please ....."

Having no luggage, Margaret and the Professor quickly found seats facing the engine and very soon their adventure was well under way. At Guildford the two people sitting near them got out, so they had plenty of room to themselves.

"Where in the concert hall are we?" asked Margaret.

"I don't know exactly, my dear. Here are the tickets. Perhaps you would like to have a look."

He handed them over and watched while she examined them. There was a number and a letter on each, but it was quite impossible to be sure without a seating plan. She was just about to hand them back, when she saw in the bottom right hand corner, £15.

"Goodness, Professor. It says here 'Ticket £15'. They must be the very best seats."

"I expect they are." he replied. "Iso appreciates the honour I do him when I give him my violin. Nothing but the best is good enough for his old tutor. Do you know, Margaret, the great Meltzac writes to me regularly each year. No matter where he may be, America, Germany, Russia, France. Every year at Christmas I get a long letter from him. And now, when he at lasts comes to England, he sends me two tickets for the very best seats, that I may once more hear the golden voice of my beloved violin."

"Did Meltzac himself send you the tickets?"

"Yes indeed."

Margaret sat quietly for a few minutes, watching the scenery fly by, thinking this over.

"It's quite an honour isn't it? To be invited to the concert by the great Meltzac himself. I mean, it makes me feel important."

The professor laughed and folded up his newspaper.

"And so you are. We both are. Now get your thing together and make sure you don't leave anything behind. We're just coming into Waterloo." And then he added mysteriously,

"I've got another surprise for you, but I'll tell you it later."

They got out of the train and after an interesting ride on the underground, they found themselves only a short walk from the concert hall. As there was still a couple of hours before the concert started, they had a walk round and then went and had some tea, Margaret all the time puzzling her brains trying to think what the new surprise could possibly be. Once inside the hall, however, she quite forgot about it in the excitement of watching the orchestra tune up. They had splendid seats. Right in the centre, a few rows from the front. She could see just about everything.

The scene was almost exactly as she had imagined it the night before. With the exception of the leader, all the members of the orchestra were in their places. Each was making sure that his or her instrument was in tune, playing little runs and trills, and the noise, not a very musical one it is true, was the sweetest sound in all the world to music lovers.

Suddenly, the audience started to clap, and Margaret said to herself – ah here comes the conductor. But she was wrong. It was the leader taking his place among the first violins. He bowed to the audience and then sat down, again the audience applauded, this time more loudly. It really was the conductor now and he acknowledged the applause with several stiff little bows. He stood by the rostrum talking to the leader for a few seconds, then, after tapping on his stand, the orchestra was playing the overture.

The applause had hardly died away after this when it started up again and rose to a perfect crescendo of hand clapping as a tall dark man, with a deep olive complexion, threaded his way very carefully between the musicians to the centre of the stage. Under his arm he held the Stradivarius violin. This was Iso Meltzac, the greatest living violinist. Margaret was so excited. The Professor was too, but for quite a different reason. Clapping as hard as she could, she gave a glance at his face, then quickly turned away. A tear glistened in his eye, as he leaned forward in his seat, to see once more the great virtuoso who had once been his pupil.

Meltzac smiled and bowed and glanced apologetically at the conductor, as the applause showed no signs of dying down. Eventually, still smiling his thanks, he held up his hand, and gradually the clapping faded away into silence. Complete quiet. Every eye in the orchestra was on the conductor, as he held his baton poised. Bows hovered expectantly over strings, then, before Margaret was aware of it, the concerto had begun. One moment there was silence, the next, the exquisite sound of muted strings crept stealthily through the quiet of the hall. She had never realised that so many instruments could play so softly. As she described to her mother later that night, it was like angel music. Just the kind of soft, beautiful music you would hear if you could see angels.

As the opening bars of the violin concerto gently unfolded, Meltzac stood motionless near the conductor, his head bowed as if in deep thought. The violin was held loosely under his arm and his bow hanging limply from his hand. The music started to swell. Muted strings sang softly, yet with ever increasing volume. The woodwind and brass harmonised so perfectly with the song of the violins that Margaret closed her eyes in rapture.

Meltzac had now lifted the violin to his chin, and stood with his bow poised over the strings. Then, as the rising crescendo of sound reached its climax, only to fade away with an abruptness which took her breath away, the golden voice of the Stradivarius took up the plaintive lament. The flashing bow of the great violinist moved swiftly over the strings. The violin seemed to come to life in his hands. It was as if the soul of the old violin maker himself had been imprisoned in the beautiful instrument, and now singing for joy at its release.

Like a lark the violin sang. Now sweet and gentle, then, as the orchestra took up the challenge, replying in tones as rich, deep and powerful as the voice of the mellowest 'cello'. With eyes closed Margaret listened as she had never listened before. On and on it went, until her heart was beating so fast with the sheer delight of it, that she thought it would never slow down again. Then, suddenly it was all over. The audience was on its feet clapping and stamping in a perfect frenzy of applause. The tall figure of Meltzac, smiling now, was bowing his thanks. Meanwhile, the conductor, completely captivated by the brilliant performance, was shaking his hand and embracing him. Even the orchestra, a smile of approval on every face, was clapping enthusiastically with the rest.

"Oh Professor, that was wonderful …..it .. well….. it was just wonderful."

The Professor, who was on his feet clapping as hard as the rest of the audience, suddenly stopped and turned to her.

"Quick Margaret, follow me. We must leave now in the interval, while they're still clapping. Meltzac has sent me a special pass and invitation to his dressing room after the performance. If we don't go now, we'll get stuck in the crowd."

So this was the other surprise. But she had not time to think, as he was already, pushing his way between the seats.

"Wait for me." she called out anxiously. She had dropped her programme and had to search under her seat. She found it, but by this time he was several yards away.

"Quickly now, Margaret." he called over his shoulder.

"I'm coming." she shouted frantically, over the din of the clapping and cheering. Energetically she pushed her way out to the aisle and just managed to grasp the outstretched hand of the Professor who was waiting for her.

It took them several minutes to reach the exit, and as the heavy door swung behind them the old man heaved a sigh of relief.

"Phew!" exclaimed Margaret. "That's better. Now which way do we go?"

They were standing in a long narrow passage which seemed to run the entire length of the hall.

"I think it's this way." answered the Professor. "If we walk to the end of the passage, we should be behind the stage. Then if we turn left, I believe the dressing rooms are on the right."

They started to walk along the passage but had not got far, when an angry voice shouted from behind,

"Hey you two. Where d'you think you're going?"

The Professor kept steadily on his way, but Margaret, looking back saw a man frantically waving his arms to them from the far end.

"Come back, come back. You're not allowed in here."

She looked nervously up at the old music master, who was still striding on not taking a scrap of notice of the shouting from behind. The voice was nearer now, and taking another peek at the angry man, she said,

"I think we'd better stop Professor. He looks very cross."

The old man did stop then, and in a very surprised manner said,

"It's quite alright Margaret, I've got a pass signed by Meltzac himself."

"Well then, perhaps you'd better show it to him, he really does look angry."

By this time, the doorkeeper, for that is who it was, had nearly caught them up, but was so out of breath he could hardly talk. All he managed to do was to wave his hands about and splutter. At last he managed to get out,

"Just where do you two think you're going? Nobody's allowed backstage. I don't know. Turn me back for half a minute and somebody sneaks in."

"Oh, we didn't sneak in. We came in to the passage from the concert hall." said Margaret.

The doorman wasn't listening.

"Now then." he shouted, wagging his finger in the Professor' face.

"Now then. Just what are you doin' 'ere. Ortergraph 'unters 'aves to wait ahtside. They aint allowed in the buildin'"

The Professor started to splutter.

"Autograph hunters! Autograph hunters!" he roared. "I'll have you know that thirty years ago, Meltzac begged for my autograph." and he wagged his finger in the doorkeeper's face.

Margaret stood alongside them and tried not to laugh. Then, pulling at the Professor's sleeve to attract his attention said,

"Don't get angry with him. Please don't get angry. Just shown him our pass."

"You're quite right. I won't waste my time getting angry with this …… this….." Without finishing, he fumbled in his pocket for the slip of paper with Meltzac's signature. Meanwhile he continued to glower at the doorkeeper, muttering,

"Autograph hunters, autograph hunters indeed!"

This made the man even more angry, but before he could utter another word, Margaret took the paper and thrust it into his hand.

"Mm." he grunted. "Admit Professor Mallais to my dressing room after the performance," he read. "signed Iso Meltzac." He stared hard at the paper and then at the Professor.

"Are you the Professor?"

"I am." snapped the Professor.

"Well, looks alright." he admitted, but still looking suspicious. Then he paused, looking at Margaret.

"Don't say anything about a young lady though, What about 'er?"

The Professor took the paper and re-read it. This was a bit of a poser. Margaret wondered anxiously what he would do. She needn't have worried. Peering ferociously over his spectacles, he said,

"Ah! Yes! ….. my ….. granddaughter. Yes, my granddaughter, Meltzac knows she is with me, but must have forgotten when he wrote this out."

"Oh Professor!" Margaret couldn't help blurting out. She was so surprised. Then to her further astonishment, the old music master turned on her fiercely and wagged his finger in her face.

"Margaret! How many times have I asked you not call me that ...... it is not seemly in two of the same blood."

The angry tone and wagging finger were belied by a broad wink he gave her and recovering from her surprise, she kept a straight face and answered meekly,

"Sorry grandfather."

For some reason this seemed to please the doorkeeper, who obviously approved of the grandfatherly discipline.

"Well," he at last said reluctantly, "I 'spose it's alright. Go straight on down, turn left and it's the third dressing room on the right."

The Professor turned and strode rapidly along the passage with Margaret chasing after him. Once round the corner he paused.

"Now, before we meet my friend Meltzac, I must apologise for giving my young pupil a new grandparent."

Margaret answered with a twinkle in her eye.

"I don't mind grandfather ..... I mean Professor. It's rather nice actually, having you for a grandfather, even if it's only for this evening. You see, I've never had one. Both mine died before I was born."

They were now standing outside the dressing room with a number three on the door. By the side of the door was a little brass bolder which held a white card. The Professor peered short-sightedly at it despite his thick spectacles. Margret came a little nearer and read aloud,

"Iso Meltzac."

She looked at the Professor.

"This is it." she said

"Yes, Margaret, this is it."

He raised his hand as though to knock, hesitated, then suddenly seemed to make up his mind.

"We will not stand on ceremony with my old pupil and friend. He would not wish it. Come, we will burst in to greet him as old friends should."

Margaret wasn't at all sure that this was a good idea, but before she could say anything, the Professor had taken her by the hand, and flinging open the door with a bang, they both tumbled into the great musician's dressing room.

Chapter 3

The Adventure Begins

Meltzac was alone in the room, standing with his back to the door when it flew open so violently. He turned round startled, then his expression changed to one of pleasure as he recognised his old tutor.

The next moment he leaped across the room and embraced the old man.

"Professor! Professor!" he cried delightedly. "My old friend Professor Mallais. Is it really you at last?"

"Iso. Iso Meltzac." was all the old music master could say, and Margaret saw his eyes suddenly dim with unshed tears, as he returned the embrace with warmth and affection.

"Indeed it is good to see you Master. I am doubly lucky today. First the magnificent audience, so warm and ready with their applause, and now a reunion with my old friend." then he caught sight of Margaret. "But come, we forget our manners, who is your so charming companion? You must introduce us."

"Do you hear him Margaret? The great Meltzac, and he still calls me 'Master'. I, whose bow now scrapes like the merest beginner ..... The greatest violinist in the world, and he still calls me 'Master'."

He looked down at his hands which were now gnarled and crippled with age, and sighed softly.

Placing his hand affectionately on the old man's shoulder, the famous violinist said quietly,

"You'll always be so to me, Professor."

Margaret couldn't help it, she had to join in.

"You're still the best teacher in the world, even if you can't play as you once did." And she looked challengingly at Meltzac, as she came forward and grasped her teacher's hand.

Meltzac smiled at her and held out his hand.

"I agree with you Margaret. So you are a violinist too?"

"Yes Mr. Meltzac," she said, shaking his outstretched hand. "I am one of the Professor's pupils."

"And one of my most promising ones too, Iso, albeit one of the youngest. Margaret is here to meet you and to see my Stradivarius violin."

"Well, I'm pleased you came. If the Professor's teaching you, you must be a very capable performer."

Margaret smiled shyly and withdrew her hand from the strong brown one holding it.

"Come Iso, the violin, the violin."

The Professor sounded just a little impatient.

"Ah yes. The violin. The incomparable Strad. See, here it is. I had not yet put it away."

He walked to the table and picked up the violin. Softly he plucked the strings with his finger, then turned and held it out to the Professor. The old man looked at it hungrily, but instead of taking it, slowly shook his head.

"Give it to Margaret, Iso. I dare not touch it. My fingers long to play it again, but I dare not. Let her hold it. Perhaps one day, she will play on my Stradivarius."

Margaret who had been gazing at the violin longingly, smiled with pleasure when she heard this.

"Oh may I hold it Mr. Meltzac? May I?"

"Of course you may. Here, take it. Hold it very gently and be careful not to drop it."

Reverently she took the beautiful instrument. For a moment she stood still, looking at it, hardly daring to breathe.

The two men smiled at each other, understanding how she felt. So, ignoring her rapt adoration, they were soon deep in conversation.

In the far corner of the room, stood a large, comfortable armchair, and Margaret moved quietly over to it and sat down, holding the violin as carefully as if it were a baby. Suddenly it seemed as though she were quite alone in the room. Oblivious of the animated talk of the two musicians, she ran her fingers up and down the strings and gazed spellbound at the exquisite workmanship of the Strad. It was difficult to believe that it had been made by old Stradivarius over two hundred and fifty years ago. The dark amber varnish was as clear and sparkling as the day it had been applied and not a scratch or blemish marred it. The magnificent scroll, perfectly carved by the great violin maker, seemed alive. Gently, she stroked the elegantly shaped body. Then, sighing contentedly, she lay back in the chair and closed her eyes.

"You beautiful, beautiful violin." she murmured softly.

Holding it tightly to her, she could almost feel the lovely melodies vibrating inside its varnished walls. Idly, she wondered about the many people who had played on it. The kind of people who had owned it throughout the two and half centuries of its existence. Who knows, she thought, even the great Nicolo Paganini himself may have once placed his fingers where hers were, on the shiny finger board. Softly she whispered,

"You beautiful violin. If only you could talk, what wonderful things you would be able to tell me."

It was then that the most surprising thing happened. The violin seemed to move gently in her arms, and a tiny voice, as sweet and clear as the music of a tinkling brook, replied,

"But I can talk. All of us can."

Margaret sat up sharply and looked down at the violin in her arms. It looked exactly the same …… or did it? Somehow, it seemed more alive. The varnish was softer and looking through one of the sound holes she could see the tiny post glowing with a faint light. Even the strings seemed to be vibrating of their own accord.

Glancing across the room to where the Professor and Iso Meltzac had been standing, she was astonished to see that they were no longer there. The room, too appeared different. It was bigger, much bigger. In fact it wasn't the same room at all. Strangely enough, she didn't feel the least bit frightened. It was very curious but not unpleasant. She glanced down at the violin again. Yes, it was different. Without thinking she tightened her grasp on the precious instrument, and as she watched, she saw the strings vibrating again and once more heard the silvery little voice. This time, however, it was higher and sharper.

"Oh! Oh! Please don't hold me so tightly. I can hardly breathe."

A faint little cough followed the words and the wood creaked alarmingly. Quickly she loosened her grip and was immediately rewarded with more sweet little sounds.

"Ah ……. thank you. That's much better."

Margaret could hardly believe her ears.

"Are you really talking, or am I dreaming?"

There came a queer little grunt of impatience.

"Do you feel as if you're dreaming?"

"Well, no I don't." she said.

"So, I must be talking to you, mustn't I?" came the pert reply.

The strings began to vibrate again, and a fat musical sigh came from the violin. Margaret actually felt it swell relax.

"It surprises me how little sense people have. Everyone knows the violin has the most beautiful voice in the world, yet although they all listen when we sing, no-one listens when we speak."

"I'll listen." said Margaret eagerly.

"I thought you would. That's why I spoke to you."

There was a pause, and she waited for the violin to speak again. When it did, it was rather unexpected.

"I think I'm going to like you, Margaret."

"And I know I'm going to like you. I love all violins, but you must be the most wonderful one in the whole world."

"Well, not quite." came the modest reply. "There are several much more famous than me. The most famous is a brother of mine. He was made just before me, but he's kept in a glass case in a museum. I expect you've heard of him. He's called the 'Messiah'."

Margaret had heard of the 'Messiah', because the Professor had told her all about it and that it was kept in a glass case in the Ashmolean Museum in Oxford. One day, she meant to go and see it.

"You were made by Stradivarius in Cremona, in Italy, weren't you?" she asked politely.

"Yes, that's right."

There was another pause, while they collected their thoughts.

"Would you like to hear about some of the people who owned me? And some of the adventures I've had with them?"

"Oh please, please." said Margaret excitedly. "Tell me about old Stradivarius first. I've often wondered what he was like."

"Ah, yes, the man who made me. He was a grand old man indeed. Do you know, Margaret, he was over eighty years old when he built me. I can see him now, in his white leather apron and soft woollen cap ....." it sighed. "It's a long time ago."

"Go on, go on, tell me about him."

"I can do better than that. I'll take you back with me into the past to watch him work. Would you like that?"

"But that's impossible." cried Margaret. "That's over two hundred years ago."

The violin shook and the tiny sound post glowed angrily as it answered.

"Alright." it said. "If you don't want to go you needn't."

"But I do, I do. I'm sorry, I didn't mean to be rude. It's just that I'm afraid I mightn't be back in time to catch my train."

The violin was silent for a moment. She watched it anxiously. In a few minutes the strings started to quiver again. The little silvery voice asked doubtfully,

"Would you really like to go? If you do you needn't worry. We'll be back in plenty of time."

"Oh, I would. Honestly I would. Goodness, this is the most exciting thing that's ever happened to me and I wouldn't miss it for anything." She grasped the violin tightly as she said this and almost immediately the little silver voice called out,

"Stop it, you're choking me. Do be careful."

Margaret moved her hand and apologised for her clumsiness.

"Well, alright, I'll forgive you this time, but violins aren't toys you know. We must always be handled with great care. We bruise very easily and I you didn't already know, we catch cold too. Always remember to wrap up your violin before putting it away in its case. Now then. Are you ready to go?"

Margaret nodded, not trusting herself to speak.

"Good. Shut your eyes then and slowly count up to a hundred. When you open them again, you will be in the workshop of old Stradivarius."

"As easily as that?"

"As easily as that. But remember, although you will be able to see and hear everything, no-one can see you. That is, of course, except me. If you want to know anything, just ask me."

Margaret closed her eyes and started to count. At thirty she heard a faint twanging of violin strings and a strange rushing sound, as if she were being carried through the air at tremendous speed. At fifty, the arms of the chair disappeared and at eighty, the comfortable padded seat changed into something extremely hard. At ninety five she heard someone whistling a lively tune and felt warm sunshine on her face and arms. Then, as she reached one hundred, the whistling became clearer and the violin vanished from her arms.

Cautiously, she opened her eyes, and gave a gasp of delight.

Chapter 4

Stradivarius' Workshop

She was sitting on the hard edge of a wooden box in the corner of a large workshop. Just in front of her was a long wooden workbench, and beyond that, the rear of a small shop with windows looking out on to a cobbled street, with the warm sunshine of an Italian summer shining through the diamond paned windows. These were made of very thick glass, pale green in colour, and with strange uneven patterns, so that the tiny houses on the other side of the street took on weird shapes as she tried to look through them.

The ceiling was low with heavy oak beams which were blackened with age. Hanging on the wall all around the workshop, were dozens of violins. A few were finished, strings and all, but most were in various stages of being made or repaired. Lying on the bench were some very unusual looking tools with sharp edges. She stood up to look at them more closely, and as she did so, a boy appeared, passed by her as if she did not exist, picked up the tools from under her nose, and whistling all the time, carried them to the far end of the workshop where he busied himself cleaning and putting them away. She stood quietly watching until he had finished. Then, he turned, walked right by her without so much as a glance, and disappeared through a door at the back of the shop.

Margaret began to look round her, this time more carefully. She had never seen so many violins in her life, and realised it was not going to be easy to find 'her' violin. They all looked so much alike. Cautiously she whispered,

"Are you there violin? Can you hear me?"

No answer. She tried again, a little louder. Still no answer. She was beginning to feel a bit worried, and started to examine them all more closely. Finally, in despair, she went back to the box and sat down again, feeling even more worried. Then, just as she wondering how she was ever going to find it, she heard footsteps, and looking at the door through which the boy had gone earlier, she saw a very old man shuffle slowly into the shop. There was no doubt as to who he was. It was the great violin maker himself, Antonius Stradivarius.

    She slipped from the box and tiptoed towards him. He was a tall thin man, with slightly bowed shoulders and dark complexion. He looked very tired. His white shirt was open at the neck and he wore dark brown britches fitted tightly just below the knee, white stockings and clumsy leather shoes with large brass buckles, one of which hung sideways. Fastened by a tape around his neck and another round his waist, was a large white leather apron, and on his head he wore a white woollen cap. In his hands he held a violin which he was examining carefully as he moved towards the bench. After a moment or two, he put it down on a piece of soft cloth and slowly shuffled out of the door again, leaving Margaret alone in the shop once more. She gazed blankly after him, then moved as if to follow out of sheer curiosity, when a tiny voice called out,

    "Well, here I am."

Startled, she turned and looked up at the row of instruments on the wall.

    "No, over here silly. On the bench."

Hurrying over, she looked down at the violin which the old violin maker had just brought in.

"Oh thank goodness I've found you." she said with relief. "You're all so much alike that if you hadn't spoken, I would never have recognized you."

"I'm not a bit like the others." it replied, sounding annoyed. "In fact, none of us is exactly alike. If you must know, I'm very special."

"Oh dear, I'm very sorry. I didn't realise."

The strings quivered and the tiny flute-like voice went on,

"In the first place, I've had fourteen coats, but I couldn't expect you to know that."

"Whatever do you mean?"

"Fourteen coats of varnish, of course. Goodness, you don't know much about violins, do you?"

"No, not as much as I thought." came the humble reply.

"Most of the instruments you see on the wall, have only seven or eight coats and a few cheaper ones a mere four. I've fourteen." it repeated proudly. Then, before she had time to say anything it went on,

"And do you know why?"

"No. But I'd like to."

"Well, first go down to the far end of the workshop, near the stairs, and open a big cupboard you'll find there. Then come back and tell me what you have seen."

She had not previously seen any stairs, but she did as she was told, and quickly found them and the cupboard. Unfastening the door, she opened it and looked inside.

Hanging on the wall were a violin, a 'cello' and two very tiny, strangely shaped violins. All were perfectly new and easily the most beautiful in the workshop. Carefully, she closed the door and went back to the bench.

"Well, what did you think of them?" the little voice asked eagerly.

"They are the most beautiful things I have ever seen." Margaret replied. Then added hastily,

"Except you, of course."

This seemed to please the violin, for the little sound post glowed and the strings vibrated happily.

"I'm one of them." it said proudly. "In fact I'm the best of the lot."

Then, literally swelling with pride, it went on,

"We have been made to the special order of the Duke of Florence, and I've just come from the drying room, the last of the five. I heard old Antonio say quite clearly to Camillo that I was the best of all. What do you think of that Margaret?"

"I think it's wonderful. You must feel very important knowing you've been specially made for a Duke. I hope I shall meet him later on when you are delivered to him."

There was such a long silence, that Margaret grew quite alarmed. Eventually with a great sigh, the violin answered,

"I'm sorry, but you won't meet him. You see, I never went to the Duke after all. All the others went, but I didn't, and I've often wondered about the lovely adventures I must have missed."

"Oh what a pity. Never mind. Just remember that if you had gone to him, you might never have been owned by Professor Mallais, and then I should never have met you."

"That's true. Still I shall never know."

Margaret hastily tried to change the subject.

"You said if there was anything I wanted to know, I was to ask you."

"Yes, that's right."

"Well, there are two questions. First, who is Camillo? You mentioned his name just now. Is he the boy I saw putting the tools away?"

"Yes. Camillo is the apprentice. You'll see him again in a moment or two. He'll be here in the shop when I start my long journey into the future. It won't be long now, for I can see the sun is going down."

Margaret didn't quite understand the bit about the sun going down, but before she could enquire, it added,

"And the next question?"

She was silent for a while, for she was reluctant to bring up the subject of the Duke again, but there seemed no other way of finding out what she wanted to know.

"When I looked in the cupboard, I saw two very small, thin violins, I've never seen funny little ones like that before."

"Ah, you mean the pair of kitts. They are miniature violins used by dancing masters. If you looked at them very closely, you'd see that although the body is very small, the neck and finger board is the same size as normal. The dancing masters play these tiny instruments while their pupils are practising. Then, if they want to show them some steps, they just put the tiny violin in their pocket, out of the way. But goodness knows why the Duke ordered them, for I'm sure he's no dancing master."

The violin breathed deeply and another great sigh escaped him.

"I really do wonder what it would have been like in the Duke's household."

"Oh, don't bother about that now. For all you know, you might have hated it."

"Perhaps you are right. I just hate not knowing." persisted the disgruntled violin.

"Listen." said Margaret suddenly. "I think someone's coming."

"Yes, it's my maker coming back. I thought we hadn't much time. Now listen carefully. As soon as you seem me leave the shop, close your eyes and count up to a hundred again. Then, when you open them you will be in my new home."

"But doesn't Mr. Stradivarius think you are to be the Duke's violin? And won't he put you away in the cupboard with the others?"

"He won't have time. Now, don't ask any more questions. Just go back and sit on the box and listen."

Quietly, she tiptoed back to her seat and waited. Soon, the old violin maker came shuffling back into the shop. He picked up the Professor's violin and ran his hands lightly and lovingly over the polished surface. As he was doing this, Camillo came back carrying some perfectly marked pieces of maple wood. He put these carefully on the bench, then looked enquiringly at his master.

"Well Camillo my boy. It is finished. The varnish is quite hard. We have now completed the instruments for His Grace."

He held the violin out at arm's length.

"It is indeed a beautiful instrument, Master."

"As yet you are no judge. But you are right Camillo. It is the finest of them all."

"There you are. What did I tell you." the tiny voice floated down from its lofty position.

The violin was being turned this way and that by the great man, being admired all the while. Then suddenly it wailed,

"Oh, why couldn't I go with the others to the Duke's palace?"

She looked quickly at the craftsman and his apprentice to see if they had noticed anything unusual. Apparently they hadn't for the old man went on,

"There isn't a better violin in the whole of Cremona. Nay, the whole of Italy."

"None better? Not even next door, husband?" a woman's voice asked playfully.

Margaret's back was turned to the staircase, so she hadn't noticed the new arrival. Neither had Stradivarius, for he said in some surprise,

"Ah Antonia, I didn't hear you come in. but in answer to your question, no, there is not a better violin in all Cremona, not even next door."

There was the faintest sound of vibrating strings from the bench.

"This is Antonia, Margaret." piped the little voice. "The old violin maker's wife. His second one" then he chuckled, "He's got thirteen children too, but thank goodness you won't see any of them, they're not allowed in the workshop."

Margaret turned and looked at the beautiful wife of old Stradivarius. Her jet black hair was drawn back tightly from her forehead, and dressed in a large knot low on the back of her neck. The heavy brocade dress she was wearing fell to the ground, held out over a small hoop, and over this she wore a black silk apron. The dress was a dark ruby red, completed by white lace drawn up to the neck, the whole making a captivating picture. She smiled and said softly,

"I don't think our neighbour Guarnarius would agree with you, husband."

The old violin maker smiled back at her.

"There are many violin makers in the Piazza St. Dominico, Antonia, but none so skilful as myself. Possibly our neighbour would not agree, for he is indeed a fine craftsman. But not even he can match the varnish used by Stradivarius." he paused, then went on,

"But come to think of it, is it not strange that the two finest violin makers in all Italy, should chance to live side by side in the same street?"

Antonia nodded her head gracefully as she said,

"Well there it is, they do, and I'm quite sure you will both agree on that. But come, it past seven o'clock and I came to call you for supper."

She half turned and took a step towards the stairs. The old man stopped her,

"Wait wife. See, here the violin which completes the concert of instruments ordered by His Grace. Is it not perfect? I can hardly bear to part with it, for His Grace plays most abominably."

Antonia came to her husband's side and gently touched the shining varnish of the Professor's violin.

"It is very beautiful Antonius. But so is this and this, and so also those that hang on the wall. And you are justly proud of them, but they are all made by your own hands, so why could you not sell His Grace one you had already fashioned? Why make a whole concert of instruments made to measure, as though they were cloaks or shirts?"

"My dear, my dear." said the old violin maker, a little shocked. "His Grace pays extra for the privilege, and it gives me great comfort to know that His Grace the Duke of Florence must have his instruments made to order by old Stradivarius of Cremona." then he added dryly, "I'm sure our neighbour Guarnarius would be only too pleased to oblige, if I were to refuse."

Camillo, who was now standing by the window, was peering through the quaintly twisted glass onto the street, and suddenly called out excitedly,

"Master, there is a customer crossing the street. He has a fiddle box under his arm and he is holding a small boy by the hand."

"Maybe he is bound for the shop of Guarnarius."

"No master. He is coming here."

Camillo ran back into the shop and stood by the workbench, next to his master. The shop bell clattered, and a short, fat man, carrying a violin case, shepherded a young boy into the shop.

"Shall I attend to him master?" whispered the apprentice pleadingly.

Antonia, who was still standing near the stairs, now called out.

"Yes, let Camillo stay and come above for your supper."

"Please." begged Camillo.

Chapter 5

The Professor's Violin is Given Away

Margaret, who was listening intently to all this, now heard the faint warning vibration of strings, so she crept a little nearer to the bench.

"This is it Margaret." said the violin. "This is the man who is going to take me away. Now don't forget what I told you to do, when you see me go."

"I won't forget." breathed Margaret softly.

Before Stradivarius could reply to Camillo's pleading, the customer came up to him and in a very pompous voice said,

"Do I address Antonius Stradivarius?"

The old violin maker turned to the little fat man and answered,

"Good day to you sir. Indeed, I am he."

"Ah ….." the little man puffed out his chest importantly. "My name is Giuseppe Franconi, and I live in Rome. This is my son."

He patted the boy on the head and continued impatiently,

"The boy, having shown some promise as a student of the violin, is shortly to have the honour to perform for Monsieur Felix Artot, the eminent violinist with a view to becoming his pupil."

The violin raised his eyebrows, but answered politely,

"I am delighted to hear it sir."

Taking a deep breath, the little man went on,

"Unfortunately, we have damaged his violin. The finger board has broken off."

He placed the case on the bench and took out the violin.

"It is a very good one. See, your name is on the label, and I am determined that none other than yourself shall repair it."

Stradivarius stroked his chin.

"My name you say? Of course, I am your service. May I see?"

The fat man smiled proudly and handed over the violin.

"Your very best work, I'm sure." he said.

Stradivarius took the violin from the stranger's fat pudgy hands and frowned sternly as he peered through one of the sound holes to read the label which was glued inside.

Margaret knew at once that something was wrong, for the old violin maker began to look very angry. She knew she was right when she heard the little voice call out,

"Look out for the fireworks Margaret. This is where the fun begins."

The great violin maker glared angrily at Signor Franconi.

"A beautiful instrument you think? Fashioned by me? Stradivarius? Pah! This varnished box sir, is a forgery. A crude apology masquerading under my Cremona label. A fake!"

He leaned over the bench and thrust the violin into the face of the startled customer and shouted,

"Some unscrupulous furniture maker, some knavish carpenter seeks to profit from the little fame which has taken me half a century to achieve."

Still shaking with anger, he held up the offending instrument to his apprentice.

"Look Camillo. The purfling. It has been inset with fire-tongs. Even you, young as you are, have better work to show."

"Yes master." said the boy, frightened by his master's temper. Poor Franconi tried to protest.

"But the label inside it. It clearly reads 'Antonius Stradivarius working in Cremona'. Could you not be mistaken?"

If anything was likely to make the violin maker even more angry, it was to cast doubt on his knowledge of violins. Still gripping the wretched violin, he waved it wildly in the air and shouted,

"Mistaken? Mistaken sir? I? Mistaken in a violin? This monstrosity is a fake I say! And I will not have it."

"Do please be careful, I beg of you." wailed Franconi. "You will damage it beyond repair."

For a moment there was pandemonium in the workshop. Stradivarius shouting angrily, Signor Franconi anxiously dancing from one foot to the other, worried for his violin, Camillo calling fearfully for his master to be careful. And if this was not enough, Franconi's young son who had been silent up to now, started to scream and stamp his feet, shouting,

"I want my violin, I want my violin."

Very faintly through the din, Margaret could hear the little silvery voice roaring with laughter. It was enjoying itself immensely.

"Damage it did you say? Damage it?" shouted the angry violin maker, as he held the violin poised over his head,

"I'll destroy it for ever. The cursed thing shall not live to mock the golden voice of my violins."

"Stop him. Stop him." screamed Franconi.

But before the horrified gaze of Signor Franconi and his wailing son, he brought the instrument crashing down on the workbench. The splintered wood flew in all directions, leaving just the neck piece in his hand.

"Ho ho ho. And that's the end of you." chuckled the Professor's violin.

There was a shocked silence. The old man, his anger spent, gazed at the broken pieces and passed a trembling hand over his forehead.

"Bring me a chair Camillo, I must sit down." Then he turned to Franconi.

"It is done and I am sorry. Truly sorry to have caused you pain sir. But the world is well rid of such trash."

Camillo placed the chair for his master and helped the tired old man lover himself onto it.

"I will call my mistress." he said, looking worried.

"Nay, do not call, I have no doubt my good wife has already heard the rumpus and is even now at the head of the stairs."

Margaret tiptoed to the stairway, and stood staring up into the shadows. Sure enough there, hidden halfway up in the gloom of the fading light, stood Antonia.

Signor Franconi was now mopping his brow and looking anxiously at his son.

"I accept your apology. But what of my son? He has no violin."

The old man wearily raised his head.

"Your son? Ah yes. Well, that is quickly remedied. Camillo. Pass me the instrument recently fashioned for the Duke."

Camillo looked at his master with a startled expression.

"But master, surely you cannot mean this one? It is part of the concert. You would not sell His Grace's violin to the first stranger who comes along." He laid his hand lovingly on the Professor's violin.

"Yes. Hand it to me boy. But I will not sell it Camillo. It is to be a gift. For I must in some measure atone for my ill manners."

The young apprentice picked it up and hugged it to his breast, as though determined it should not leave the building.

"No! No! Master you must not do it. You have worked five weary months on it and it's one of your best. You can't give it away now."

Margaret heard the creaking of the stairs and guessed that Antonia was on her way down to join them.

"Come, come lad." came the gentle reply. "Give it to me, for make a present of it I will, and maybe the boy will be worthy of it, for the Duke certainly is not."

Camillo seemed heartbroken.

"Oh master, master." he cried and turning towards the stairs ran straight into the arms of Antonia, where they stood in the darkened doorway, she with her arms round the sobbing boy.

"He is a good lad." sighed old Stradivarius. "He loves all the instruments we create, even as I do myself. Here sir, treat it well. Wrap it up carefully and put it in the case." This done, he shuffled once more to his chair and sank down exhausted.

"I am overwhelmed by your generosity sir. My thanks. It will be looked after well, never fear."

A few minutes later, the violin case held securely under his arm, Signor Franconi was anxious to be gone. He grasped his small son by the hand and said hurriedly.

"We must be on our way. It grows dark, and in a strange town I am at a loss. Good day sir."

"Good day to Signor. Take care of my violin."

The door closed with a clanging of bells and the Professor's violin had started its wonderful journey into the future.

Margaret got up from her box but sat down abruptly when she realised that Antonia was standing right beside her.

"Well husband?"

The tired old man looked up wearily at the sound of her voice.

"Is it you, wife? Do not worry, I am tired, that is all."

Speaking very gently, Antonia replied,

"Of course you are tired husband, and for a very good reason. You grow old and such outbursts of temper cannot be indulged in without immediate payment."

"Yes, you are right my dear." then he humbly added.

"I'm sorry, but this the third time I have detected a forgery in the last two months and I worry whether there are more out there under a false label, hoping to sully the name of Stradivarius."

"Never mind Antonius. To copy is but to praise. More importantly, what can we say to the Duke's messenger when he arrives?"

"I know not. Perhaps Camillo, you can think of something?"

Camillo , who was lighting the candles, looked up eagerly at his master.

"Ah. A new violin must be born, is that it Camillo?" he said, smiling at the boy. Camillo nodded and ran off happily, bringing back some new choice wood – figured maple – and then dragged the heavy violin moulds up to the bench ....

Antonia watched these preparations in silence, then said kindly, but firmly,

"But first your supper husband. Then you must rest. Tomorrow will be soon enough. You Camillo can leave your work now and let your master have his rest. Come husband, for not another moment's delay will I allow."

Leaning heavily on his wife's arm, the grand old violin maker walked slowly up the steep staircase, but could not resist calling over his shoulder,

"In one hour I will be back."

The laughing voice of the young apprentice came floating up from somewhere in the cellar.

"Yes, master. In one hour."

A door banged at the top of the stairs and Margaret realised that she was once more alone in the workshop.

In the flickering candlelight she took one final look round and whispered softly

"Goodbye Mr. Stradivarius. Goodbye Antonia. Goodbye Camilo."

Then she closed her eyes and slowly started to count.

Chapter 6

The Soul of the Violin

When next she opened her eyes, she got quite a nasty shock. She couldn't see a thing. It was pitch dark and the only thing she was sure about was that she was sitting on a very soft chair. For one terrible moment she thought she was back in Iso Meltzac's dressing room, and that they had gone home and forgotten all about her. Even the old violin maker's candlelit workshop was better than this. Sitting there alone in the dark and silence of a strange place, she began to feel frightened.

"Are you .....are you there, violin?" she whispered cautiously.

To her great relief, she heard its now familiar voice, although this time indistinct and muffled, but the sound quickly restored her confidence.

"Where are you?" she said softly. "It's so dark in here, I can't see a thing."

"I'm in my case, on a shelf right in front of you." answered the little voice. "Put out your hand and undo the case, then we can talk properly."

She easily found the case, and after fumbling for a moment or two, she undid the catches and lifted the lid. A sweet musical sigh rewarded her.

"Ah, that's better. Now we can talk."

As she pulled the silk scarf away from it, the tiny sound post glowed its approval. In fact, it was so bright she could now see it plainly, and a part of the room in which she was sitting.

"Oh!" groaned the violin. "I have had a terrible time."

"Have you? Why what's happened?"

"It's that boy. He plays so badly, he makes my head ache. Day after day, scrape, scrape. I shall be glad to move on."

"What do you mean? Day after day? You've only been here an hour or so."

"Don't be silly Margaret." the violin answered scathingly. "I've been here nearly a year."

"B...but I don't understand. It seems only a few minutes ago we were in the workshop where you were made."

"Oh, time means nothing on this journey with me." said the violin airily, "In fact, when we've finished talking, and you count again, it will be more than a hundred years later when you open your eyes."

Margaret was silent for a while, thinking this out. It was all very puzzling. But before she could say anything, the violin spoke again.

"Actually, nothing much happens to me in the next fifty years or so." it said. "In a week from now, I get stolen, and I'm sold to a collector of rare violins."

"That sounds interesting."

"It isn't. You see, the collector knows I've been stolen, and is afraid to show me to anyone. So he locks me away in his house, and there I stay, until he dies. Mind you, fifty years isn't long in the life of a violin. Anyway after that I was sold again, and then again and nobody seemed to remember that I'd been stolen."

"Did anyone important buy you?"

"Yes. And it was just about the most important thing that ever happened to me. You see, I was finally bought by the Count de Cesole, a French nobleman."

"What happened then?" asked Margaret.

"The really important thing was that he was a very close friend of the greatest violinist who ever lived."

"Nicolo Paganini." breathed Margaret, softly.

"Ah. So you know something about violins and violinists." said the violin in some surprise.

"Of course I do. And I shall know a lot more by the time I get home, thanks to you. But did Paganini ever play on you?"

"He did. Several times in fact." was the proud reply.

Margaret looked at the Professor's violin with even more respect than before. To think that the great Paganini had held and played it. She picked it up and ran her fingers gently over the fingerboard.

"Now that's better." it said. "I hardly felt a thing that time. You're learning."

The two were silent for a moment in the darkness. Then,

"Can I ask you two questions?"

"Fire away." said the violin jauntily.

"When I look at you, especially now, in the dark, I can see your sound post glowing and it does it even more when you speak. It gives me a lovely feeling too, why is that?"

The violin was silent for such a long time, Margaret thought that perhaps she had upset it. When it did speak, it was in a low serious tone.

"I know what you feel, because I feel it too, but I don't know why. I only know that the sound post is the most important part of us. Without it, we're only a queer shaped box with strings, but with no life, no voice."

Margaret looked at it wonderingly.

"Oh yes." it went on. "I remember when I was made, my maker was very, very careful when he fitted my sound post. It took him several days, but when he got it just right, I knew I was born. I knew even without trying that I could sing like an angel."

"But why does it glow?"

"I can't explain that either. I can only tell you that Stradivarius is said to have loved all of us so much that he placed a little piece of his soul in each one. It may be true, or may not, but it is a fact that in France, they always call the sound post 'the soul of the violin', so perhaps there is some truth in it."

"True or not," said Margaret, "I think it's a lovely story."

Again they sat silently in the darkness. As the violin stopped talking, the glow faded and the night enveloped them once more like a black cloak. After a while, it called out briskly,

"Well, what is your second question?"

"Can't you guess?" she teased.

"Ah, of course, you want to know if you are going to see Paganini?"

"Yes. Am I?" Margaret asked eagerly.

"That's exactly what I've got planned for your next adventure. When next you open your eyes, we'll be in France, and you will see ..... what you will see." it finished mysteriously.

"When can we start?" asked Margaret excitedly.

"There's plenty of time." the violin sighed and relaxed. "I'm enjoying our chat."

"Where are we?" said Margaret suddenly. "In Signor Franconi's house in Rome?"

"Yes."

"Couldn't I see something of Rome while I'm here?"

"Don't be silly." said the violin sharply, "It's two o'clock in the morning and everybody will be in bed."

A moment later, another thought struck her.

"Did Paganini play on you at any of his concerts?"

"Good gracious no!" came the reply. "Didn't you know, Paganini always played on a Guarnarius violin after he became famous? You remember? Guarnarius who lived next door to old Stradivarius?"

"Were his violins better?"

"Certainly not. It just so happened that Paganini had a Guarnarius given to him when he lost his own through gambling, and he was so grateful, that he swore never to play on anything else."

"It must have been a very beautiful instrument. Where is it now?"

"I can tell you that. If you mean where is it in your own time."

"Of course." laughed Margaret. "That's what I meant. Where will it be when I get back to my own century."

"Well, when he died, it was found that he willed his violin to his birthplace, Genoa. And that's where it still is, in a glass case, together with his bow, for all to see."

"Perhaps I can go there one day to see it."

"Yes. Of course it's not as good as looking at me."

Margaret smiled to herself in the dark.

"Come along then." said the violin in a business-like manner. "Time we were moving. Put me in my case, and then you know what to do."

Very carefully, she wrapped it up in its silk scarf and put it gently back in the case, closing the lid and doing up the clasps. Then she sat back in her comfortable chair and started to count. As she did so, she couldn't help wondering what it would feel like to leap ahead one hundred years. She needn't have worried. This time there was no kind of feeling at all.

Chapter 7

Nicolo Paganini

With eyes tightly closed, Margaret continued to count. As she reached ninety one, the faint sound of violin music came to her ears. The moment she got to a hundred, she knew that a violin was being played brilliantly, quite close to her.

During those first few seconds, she found it difficult to keep her eyes open, for she was sitting facing a window and strong sunlight was shining on her face. Gradually she got used to the light and the very first thing she noticed was that she was sitting, this time, in an elegant high backed chair. Her back was to the room and she was gazing through the window down onto a beautiful avenue of trees. People were passing to and fro, and away in the distance she could see the blue of the sea sparkling in the sunshine. She did not know it, of course, but she was sitting in a magnificent bedroom of a villa in Nice in the south of France.

Suddenly the music stopped and a harsh voice growled fretfully,

"To the devil with the sawbones who keeps me chained to this miserable sickbed."

Startled, Margaret turned to see where the voice was coming from. That was when, for the first time, she realised she was in the largest, most beautiful room she had ever seen in her life. The walls were hung with rich tapestries, the floor was covered with the thickest of carpets and the most delicate and elegant furniture was dotted about. She drew in her breath and gasped in wonder, when she saw the enormous bed with its silken hangings, which occupied the centre of the room. Never had she seen such a bed. At least six or seven people could have slept there. Four carved posts extended high above the bed itself, and a huge canopy of richly coloured silk covered it, making it look more like a silken caravan than a bed. Heavy brocade curtains covered with a strange foreign design in gold and silver were drawn back at the sides and ends and held in position by thick ropes of twisted silk. Sitting in solitary state in this gilded magnificence, completely dwarfed by the splendour of his surroundings, was Nicolo Paganini, the greatest violinists of all time.

    Margaret recognised him at once, from pictures in a book that Professor Mallais had once leant her. The hooked nose, pointed chin, long bony face and the piercing black eyes, now dulled by illness, made her certain. On his head he wore a woollen night cap with a silk tassel which dangled by his ear. As she watched, he gave a huge sigh, closed his eyes and leant back on the pillows. The violin which he had been playing lay neglected across his chest, and the bow dangled limply from his hand over the edge of the bed. Margaret got up and moved to where she could see him more clearly.

    Suddenly, he sat up in the bed again, thrust the violin under his chin and vigorously drew the bow across the strings. His huge left hand with its tapering fingers moved swiftly over the finger board and a cascade of bell-like notes filled the big bedroom. There seemed to be no tune, just a succession of notes which reminded her of a waterfall on an early summer's morning. Abruptly, the music stopped, and she heard him murmur self pityingly,

    "I think I really must be ill."

Then the bow swept over the strings again and a lovely melody sang round the room.

So this was the magic of the master violinist, of whom she had read. A violinist whose talent was such that some people said he must have sold his soul to the devil, to be able to play as he did. But Margaret knew in her own heart as she listened to the lovely refrain, that this could not possibly be true. Such music could only be inspired by thoughts that were good. A moment later, the exquisite melody faded into nothing once again.

"I am but a shadow of myself." the great violinist murmured forlornly.

Then he stirred once more. This time a lilting tune. This was the music she loved best of all. The kind of happy, laughing music that made you think of fairy folk dancing. Deep in the heart of some secret wood, she could see the little people whirling and twirling to the magic of Paganini's violin. Faster and faster it sang. Quicker and quicker they danced ..... then the door opened, and the spell was broken. Quickly, she went back to her chair by the window, turning it round so that it faced the room. As she sat down, she heard the man on the bed say,

"So you've come back at last."

He was speaking to an elegantly dressed gentleman who had just entered the room. It was the Count de Cesole, rich friend and patron of the sick man. Margaret looked with awe at his striped waistcoat, tight trousers and black silk neck-cloth which he wore as a cravat tied round a high winged collar, a high crowned beaver hat, and under his arm a strange shaped parcel. He threw his hat carelessly on to a small table which stood nearby, then strolled over to the bed. He put the parcel on the foot of it and taking the violin and bow gently from his friend's limp hand said,

"I'll be bound you've been playing all afternoon."

Paganini shrugged his thin shoulders eloquently.

"Playing you call it?" He leaned back and closed his eyes.

"I shall never play in public again, Cesole. My hand has lost its cunning. My violin no longer sings for me."

"You are ill my dear friend, and of course, your performance suffers a little. But soon, you will be better, and once again the violin will sing for you."

Paganini wearily opened his eyes.

"Tell me. Am I so very ill? How long will I have to lie here in this bed of yours? Tell me truly Cesole. On your heart. Am I likely to die?"

Margaret could see the pain in the Count's eyes, as he lowered them before the gaze of his stricken friend. Speaking very gently he replied,

"It is true Nicolo you are ill, and I would not keep it from you, but the doctor is sure that if you do as he says, you will be up and about again in a few weeks."

Paganini looked at him searchingly. Then, closing his eyes once more he said,

"You are indeed a true friend, but I am not deceived."

The Count suddenly straightened up.

"Away with this morbid mood. See, I've something here which will chase away your gloom."

With the merest suspicion of a smile, the sick man looked at the parcel on the bed.

"I must confess, I was a little intrigued by the parcel." he said.

The Count began to take off the wrappings, while the invalid watched the mysterious movements with interest.

"It is, of course, another violin for your collection."

"Your guess is correct, as usual. But what a violin! Just wait until I show you."

Several pieces of coloured cloth were now spread over the bead, and Paganini sat up in anticipation.

"Let me see it, my friend. What a marvellous instrument is this that needs the swaddling clothes of an infant. Not another wrapping surely?"

"Just one more. Ah, you will see here something to rival your beloved Guarnarius, Nicolo?"

"Never. Unless it be by another hand." came the cool reply.

The Count laughed, whirled away the final covering and said,

"There, name it, before I place it in your hands."

"Undoubtedly a Stradivarius." came the instant answer. "Yes, most certainly a Stradivarius. The scroll is enough. I need look no further. You are to be congratulated Cesole. This is indeed the work of Antonio Stradivarius of Cremona. Superb!"

Margaret now silently crossed the room so that she could see more clearly. It was the Professor's violin, of course. The tiny glow, which only she could see, was proof enough.

"Hello Margaret." said a sweet little voice.

"Hello violin." she whispered back.

Softly she crept back to her seat.

The Count was quite excited.

"See, the arching of the back. And the varnish Nicolo. Do you note the varnish?"

"See how the light reflects, as from a jewel." breathed the Count.

"An instrument such as this is a jewel, my friend." Then, running his hand lovingly over the back of the violin, added softly, "Ah …..Maple and pine. No better combination Cesole. Figured maple and close grained pine." Abruptly he put it down among the covers.

"And what of its history? Such violins as this are not to be had for the asking."

Cesole sat on the edge of the bed and told him.

"Purchased by my agent from the effects of Gaspare the violinist, who bought it a few months before he died, from the Italian collector, Bacuzzi."

"So. Gaspare has gone." Paganini smiled to himself. "Ah well! He was never more than fair." he added ungraciously. "I wonder how he managed to persuade Bacuzzi to part with it, for it must have been the gem of his collection." mused the violinist thoughtfully.

"There was no difficulty about that, Nicolo. Bacuzzi too is dead and Gaspare happened to be the highest bidder at the sale. It was whispered that the wily old collector bought it years ago from someone who bought it from an old down at heel musician who, so the tale goes, stole it from a young boy, who had it from old Stradivari himself as a gift."

"A pretty story, but whether true or not, I'm sure it increased the price. But come., hand me my bow. We will see if its voice is as heavenly as its appearance."

"Have you not played enough for today? You must not get too tired." said the Count, concerned for his friend.

Paganini, however, was not to be put off.

"Do not fuss, my friend." he said impatiently, and sat himself higher up in the bed, beckoning to Cesole to hand him the violin and bow.

Cesole sigh resignedly.

"As you will Nicolo."

He handed the bow to this friend and sat down again by the bedside. Margaret too, got up and crossed the room to stand on the opposite side. She was determined not to miss anything. The sound of tuning filled the room.

"Huh! It promises well."

The master violinist with the magic fingers, swept his bow over the strings and produced a series of flute like sounds which reminded her of thistle down dancing over the fields in a summer breeze.

"Superb!" breathed the Count.

Then, without warning, Paganini drew his bow smoothly and delicately across the G string and started to play the beautiful melody which Margaret had heard him play earlier. Later on, she would recognise the sad, haunting tune as part of Paganini's own composition: the Napoleon Sonata for G String. This time he played it right to the end, and for half an hour, Margaret and the Count were held spellbound by the magic of the great virtuoso. Finally, the deep, rich tones faded into silence, and the Count, overcome by emotion, placed his hand on his friend's shoulder and murmured,

"A heavenly melody, a master hand and a perfect violin."

Completely exhausted, the great violinist lay back with his eyes closed. Gently, his friend took the instrument and bow from him and placed them on a nearby velvet covered table, then he went to the foot of the bed, picked up the Guarnarius violin and laid it by the side of the Stradivarius.

Leaving the bedside, Margaret quietly went back to her chair by the window, and waited to see what would happen next. The Count was rearranging the pillows and after smoothing the rumpled covers, he bent low over the sick man and whispered,

"Get some sleep Nicolo. I'll come back later."

The room was now quite quiet, except for the invalid's breathing and the steady ticking of the huge gold and marble clock which stood in the centre of the great mantelpiece over the fireplace.

Patiently, Margaret waited, and after a little while she heard the now familiar buzz of vibrating strings.

Chapter 8

Some Interesting Conversations

The strange little vibrations continued for some minutes, then she heard a few tinkly notes coming from the table just as she expected. She stood up, waiting for 'her' violin to start speaking to her, but instead, an angry voice called out,

"Well, what do you mean by it?"

She stood still in surprise. Then the Professor's violin answered.

"What do I mean by what?" it said.

Margaret put her hand to her mouth in astonishment, and sat down again quickly. The two violins were talking to each other!

"What do you mean by coming here and stealing my master's affections?"

"But I didn't. I haven't." came the reply.

"Oh yes you did. I heard you. Singing for him. No other violin in the world but me has ever sung as well as that."

"Can I help it if I'm one of the best violins in the world." said the Stradivarius smugly.

"Oh, you are, are you?" replied the Guarnarius fiercely. Then added,

"All right then. Go on, who were you made by?"

"Antonius Stradivarius." very proudly came back the reply.

There was a short silence. Then in a more friendly tone, it said,

"That makes us kind of cousins, I suppose. I was made by Guarnarius, who lived next door."

"Hmm." it said doubtfully. "Maybe it does. Anyway, we mustn't quarrel, for I'm sure your voice is quite as good as mine, and I don't expect your master will play on me again for ages."

"That's very nice of you. About my voice I mean. Considering you've never heard me."

"Everyone knows that your maker and mine are the best violin makers in the world, so it follows that you must have a beautiful voice. Anyway, stands to reason, Paganini wouldn't own you if you didn't."

Margaret was sitting listening to all this and now decided to join in.

"Have you forgotten me?" she said.

"Who's that?" said the Guarnarius sharply. For a few seconds there was a lot of whispering coming from the table. Then there was a soft laugh and both violins started to chuckle at a private joke. Margaret walked over to them and looked down sternly.

"I do hope you're not laughing at me."

A burst of fairy like laughter answered her, then the Professor's violin, still shaking with repressed giggles, replied,

"I was just telling my cousin here some of the things you don't know. He thought it was very funny."

"Well, I think you're both very rude."

There was a silence for a moment and all that could be heard was the ticking of the clock and the breathing of the sleeping Paganini. Margaret waited. Finally, in a small, rather ashamed voice, 'her' violin said,

"I'm sorry Margaret. I didn't mean to be rude."

"I'm sorry too." added the other violin.

"All right. I forgive you both." she said and laughed.

She was rewarded by a fascinating cascade of silvery notes which tumbled over one another in their eagerness to be heard. Then she added.,

"But I think you both should be taught a lesson!"

"Oh?" said the two little voices, blankly.

"Yes. So I'm going to test your knowledge of violins by asking one question."

"Oh good. We know all there is to know about violins."

"Do you? We'll see. Now, be quiet while I think."

She pretended to think hard for a minute or two, then said,

"Just see if you can answer this one."

"Go on then. We're ready."

"How many separate parts of pieces of wood are needed to make a violin?"

"That's easy" said the Guarnarius quickly. "Twenty."

"You're guessing." said Margaret sternly. "And you're wrong."

"Oh!.....Thirty then."

"You're still guessing, and still wrong."

Somewhat abashed, it said no more. Meanwhile, the Professor's violin had started to count aloud.

"Six pieces for my ribs, one for my front, two for my back, that's nine." There was a moment's silence then the little voice continued somewhat doubtfully,

"I make it forty three …. no thirty three. Oh dear, it comes out different each time I do it. Every time I come to my corner blocks I can't remember if I counted my ribs."

Margaret laughed.

"So you give up? Neither of you know?"

"Not really – unless it's forty?" said the Guarnarius hopefully.

"Wrong again. Now, let this be a lesson to you both. You don't know as much as you think you do."

All this time the Professor's violin was still struggling to count its pieces, but finally gave up in despair.

"I don't know Margaret, how many are there?"

"Seventy two." said Margaret distinctly.

Both instruments were silent while they thought this one out.

"I don't feel like seventy two separate pieces."

"Neither do I."

"Of course you don't." put in Margaret. "You feel like one piece, and that's the difference between a good violin and a poorly made one. A skilful craftsman is so careful in putting all the bits together that it's sometimes impossible to see the joins."

"And are we like that?"

"Certainly. You were made by the two most brilliant violin makers in the world." She waited a little while, looking down on them both, then went on,

"Now I want to ask you some real questions. Since hearing you both sing so beautifully, I want to know what happens to both of you next. What happens to you after the Professor's violin and I leave you to go on with our adventures?"

"Nothing much, I'm afraid." murmured the Guarnarius sadly. "You see Margaret, my poor master is very ill indeed. In fact he never gets better. When he's gone, I feel I never want to sing again. Perhaps that's as well, for they take me home to Italy and put me in a glass case in Genoa where my poor master was born, and there I stay. In fact, I'm still there when we reach the century in which you live. When you're older, perhaps you can come and visit me." it finished wistfully.

"I will, I certainly will." she promised.

"Would you like to hear how Paganini came to own me?"

"I have heard something about it, but please tell me."

"Well, when Nicolo Paganini was a young man, everyone idolised him and I'm afraid success went to his head. For a time he lived a very wild life. Drinking and gambling, you know."

Margaret nodded sympathetically.

"One day he wagered his violin and lost it. The next day he was due to play in a concert and in despair because he had no money to buy a new one. I was the finest violin in the collection of a wealthy Italian nobleman who, on hearing of the young Paganini's troubles, offered to lend me to him. After the concert, when Paganini tried to return me, he was so amazed and delighted by the young man's playing, he gave me to him. My warm hearted master was so overcome by this unexpected generosity that he swore he would play only on me for the rest of his life. He kept his promise, but soon we shall be parted for ever." it finished sadly.

"It's a beautiful story, and I'll never forget it." said Margaret softly. Then she added, "And I really will come and see you in Italy someday. That's my promise."

They were all quiet again for another few minutes. At last the Professor's violin piped up with,

"Any more questions then?"

"Oh yes. I'd like to know what happens next. To us I mean."

"Well, let me see. I just stay in the Count's collection and am brought out at intervals to be admired by his friends. They all say how wonderful I am……"

"Don't boast." put in the Guarnarius.

"It's true!"

"Even if it is, there's no need for you to say it."

The Stradivarius looked at his companion coldly and went on,

"As I was saying. I'm with the Count, and when he dies, I stay with his son and the same thing happens, I'm much admired by all." it said, looking cheekily at the other violin.

"Bah!" snorted the Guarnarius.

"Go on." said Margaret. "What happens after that?"

"Then I'm sold by auction to an unscrupulous Italian dealer."

"How old will you be when I see you next?"

"Oh ..... about a hundred and thirty or so I think. I'm not quite sure. Time passes so quickly for a violin."

"Ssh! Listen!" interrupted the Guarnarius. "I can hear someone coming. It's the Count."

"Yes." said Margaret. "I can hear footsteps too."

"We'd better say goodbye then." whispered the Professor's violin. Don't forget what you have to do."

"I'm not likely to do that." she replied. Then, touching the silky varnish of the Guarnarius violin with her finger tips, she whispered to it,

"Goodbye, I'll see you again someday. I promise."

The footsteps were nearer now.

"Goodbye Margaret. We'll be meeting again soon."

"Goodbye violin."

She blew a kiss to them both and crossing the room, sat down by the window again. She closed her eyes and was starting to count again just as the door opened, so she did not see the Count enter the room on tiptoe, pick up both violins and leave the room with them.

Chapter 9

The Market Place

When next she opened her eyes, it was the strangest awakening she had ever experienced. There was no comfortable seat this time. She was standing in the middle of a small market place. Little wooden stalls were set up in rows all round her. Each was laden with something different. One was groaning under the weight of a load of cabbages. Then there were apples, pears, plums. cherries and other fruit. Carrots, turnips, onions, potatoes and eggs. One, quite close to her, had piles of plates, cups, beakers and saucers, all painted in the brightest colours. On a box, by the side of his stall, sat an old man wearing wooden sabots on his feet, dirty pantaloons tied at the ankle and a faded loose blouse which had once been blue, but was now covered with the many different colours of the paint he was using to decorate his wares. He was holding a plate in his hand and carefully painting dainty little forget-me-nots all round the edge.

People were passing between the stalls, and every now and then, someone would stop in front of one of them. Immediately the stall holder would leap up and straight away, what sounded like an argument would start. At last the customer would depart with a dozen eggs, or a pound of butter or maybe a large cabbage, but neither buyer nor seller ever seemed satisfied with the transaction. Both seemed convinced he had the worst of the bargain.

Margaret watched, quite fascinated, and then began to wander round the market, not knowing what else to do. She was looking for a sign of the Professor's violin, but without success. Soon, finding herself on the edge of the market place, she crossed the cobbled street and stood disconsolately outside a baker's shop. The appetizing smell of freshly baked bread wafted up to her from a small grill below the window, reminding her suddenly how hungry she was, and she was just thinking how nice it would be to taste a hot piece of bread covered in lovely deep yellow butter like she had seen on one of the stalls, when a short dark man with a pointed black beard came across the street and stood outside the shop as though waiting for someone.

She looked at him closely, but couldn't recognise him or connect him with the violin. She was just about to move away, when two more men came hurrying along, stopped outside the shop and started to talk to the first man. One of them had a violin case strapped to his back. Margaret moved closer so that she could hear what they were saying. The man with the beard spoke first.

"Your instructions are clear, Pierre?"

"Yes Monsieur. Half an hour before the sale begins, I am to mingle with the buyers, and spread the word that the violin is not genuine. I am to hint that I heard that Monsieur is not bidding for that reason."

"Good. I shall be there, of course, but I shall not bid."

He then turned to the man with the violin case.

"Now, you Henri. What is your part in this little comedy?"

Henri grinned stupidly, showing blackened teeth.

"I shall ape the country bumpkin Monsieur, with a passion for fiddles."

"That'll be easy!" snorted Pierre.

Henri looked up enquiringly, but was too dense to see the point of the remark. He grinned again, and tapped the case on his back, as the bearded man said sharply,

"Enough Pierre. Be quiet. Go on Henri."

"With the fiddle box under my arm, I shall enter the sale room just before the violin is offered and when there is no bid, I shall offer one hundred centimes. But first I look in my pockets to see what I am worth. That will look good and genuine, eh Monsieur?"

The bearded man smiled cunningly.

"Yes." he agreed. "If you do it properly."

"And the money, Monsieur?"

It was Pierre speaking now.

"You'll get it when you deliver the violin to me."

"Ah, but the hundred centimes. You will give Henri that? We are poor. We have barely a few sous between us."

After a moment's hesitation, the man with the beard reluctantly counted out the coins into Henri's grimy paw. Pierre watched the money disappear into his companion's pocket with undisguised jealousy.

With a final warning to do exactly as he had told them, the bearded one started to turn away, then added,

"Never fear, you will be rewarded handsomely if I have the violin in my hands by this evening."

With that he walked briskly off in the direction of the market place and was soon lost in the crowd.

Margaret decided to follow him. If he was going to a sale, surely that would be where she would find the violin. Henri and Pierre would be there too. Now, although she did not realise it, she was following Luigi Tarisio, an Italian, who for many years had devoted his life to the search for rare violins. He had no conscience at all and always got what he wanted – usually, dishonestly – and seemed to have a flare for finding valuable violins in the most unexpected places. A favourite trick of his was to offer a bright, shiny new violin in exchange for an old one, knowing he was getting the best of the bargain, and in this way he got many rare and valuable instruments, which he later sold at high prices, making a handsome profit.

With Margaret at his heels, he pushed his way through the crowded market place and entered a shop. Looking through the window, she saw him sit down at a table and start talking to a man with an apron on. He was going to have a meal. Keeping her eye on the door, she strolled back to the market and stood watching the colourful scene. It was just like a picture from her history book at school. After a while, she realised the crowds were getting more dense and she was afraid she might lose sight of the man with the black beard, so she turned back to the shop. It was just as well she did, for she had barely crossed the cobbled street once more, when she saw him leave and turn into the side street nearby.

Keeping close behind him, she found they had not far to go. Emerging from the alley, the violin dealer paused in front of a large, fine looking building. It was quite different from the little shops and houses she had seen all round the market place. Marble steps led up to an imposing doorway, which was flanked by two enormous statues. The door was open and as Tarisio passed into the entrance, Margaret could hear the murmur of voices.

Curiously, she followed her unwitting guide, and found herself in a very large hall. Oil paintings covered the walls, and the floor was completely covered with furniture of all kinds. Chairs, tables, inlaid writing desks, linen presses and beds by the dozen. At the far end was a platform and on this stood a man. In front of him was a narrow table and he was waving a wooden hammer. All around him people were gathered.

"Going! Going! Gone!" he called out, as he brought down his hammer onto the table with a bang.

"Why, it's an auction sale." whispered Margaret to herself.

Threading her way through the pieces of furniture, she looked eagerly round, but still saw no sign of 'her' violin, although she felt sure it must be here somewhere.

The auctioneer was asking for bids for a chest of drawers, but Luigi Tarisio was not interested in furniture apparently, for he stood chatting to a small group of men in a far corner of the hall, none of whom were paying any attention to what was going on. When the chest was finally sold, there was a pause. Most of crowd had wandered off, but other small groups who so far had not taken any part in the bidding, now moved in close to the auctioneer's table. Tarisio moved also, and was now standing quite alone with his back to the auctioneer, examining a painting.

The auctioneer cleared his throat with a dry little cough, adjusted his spectacles and said,

"We now come to the musical instruments, gentlemen."

Reaching down into the depths under his table, he produced a violin.

Chapter 10

Dirty Dealings at the Auction

The dealers edged nearer as the auctioneer continued.

"Today we are very fortunate to have four very fine violins by famous makers. All, at one time, the property of the late Count de Cesole, well known collector of rare violins."

He paused and beamed at the little group below him. It was just at that moment that Margaret caught sight of Pierre. He was whispering to one of the dealers. As she watched he passed from one to the other. One or two of the men he spoke to smiled wisely, others frowned, and one old gentleman looked round searchingly until he saw Tarisio who was still looking at one of the paintings on the other side of the hall, apparently not taking the slightest interest in the proceedings.

The old gentleman then walked over to another man and the two held a whispered conversation, turning now and then to watch Tarisio, who with a glass to his eye was examining the picture inch by inch.

"Now gentlemen." the auctioneer continued. "The first on my list is a beautiful instrument by Jacobus Stainer. Even to my untrained eye, it is a magnificent specimen. What am I bid?"

The old gentleman lifted his hand and called,

"One hundred."

"And fifty." swiftly put in another voice.

"Two hundred." said the old gentleman.

"Three." added a third voice.

"And fifty." This time slowly from the old gentleman.

"Four hundred and fifty."

The new voice came from the back of the hall, and Margaret turned round with the rest to see who spoke.

Tarisio was seated on an elaborately carved chair with the painting in his hands.

"It is my only bid." he apologised with a smile directed at the other dealers. A murmur filled the room as the auctioneer repeated the bid and called for more.

"Ah. Tarisio is here. The rogue will sell his soul for a rare violin."

This whispered remark reached Margaret's ears and she listened hard for the muttered reply.

"Rogue he may be, but certainly he knows a good fiddle when he sees one. If he's willing to pay four hundred and fifty francs, you may be sure it's worth twice that." Then he shouted,

"I bid five hundred."

"And fifty." came plaintively from the old gentleman.

"That's Jaubert from Paris." whispered one of those who had not yet bid.

"Confound him." said his companion under his breath. "He's bidding well over my limit, as usual."

At last, the bidding finished, the auctioneer finally called out,

"Going! Going! Gone!" and brought his hammer down with a resounding bang. He then reached down once more into the darkness by his side.

"Just like a magician taking a rabbit out of a hat." smiled Margaret to herself,

"The next item is a violin by Antonius Stradivarius working in Cremona about 1730." he now called out.

Margaret moved in closer, and saw to her relief, that here at last was the Professor's violin.

Pierre, still intent on his whispering campaign round the dealers was saying,

"This one is the fake. This is the one. I heard Tarisio tell a friend. Do not bid Monsieur. He will not bid for it. You will see."

The dealers had now broken up into little groups and were talking in whispers.

"See." said one. "The rumours must be true. Tarisio isn't interested in the Strad. He's not even looking at it. I, for one, shan't bid."

"Nor I."

"Nor I." A chorus of agreement came from the listeners.

The auctioneer cleared his throat once more.

"Come gentlemen. Your bids please."

There was much shuffling of feet but no reply.

"What? Do none of you wish to possess this perfect instrument?"

A faint murmur of dissent rippled through the crowd, and Margaret caught sight of the cunning smile on Pierre's face, as he slowly moved from group to group, poisoning their minds against the beautiful Stradivarius.

"Why does not Tarisio bid?" suddenly a voice called out.

All eyes turned to the bearded dealer at the back of the hall. He smiled, shrugged his shoulders and went back to examining the paintings.

"The cunning dog knows something." whispered someone.

The auctioneer tried again.

"Will no-one bid me even one hundred to start us off?"

Margaret could see Luigi Tarisio was now standing nervously pulling at his pointed beard, although she saw the gleam of triumph in his black beady eyes. Now was the time for Henri to arrive and both he and Pierre glanced anxiously at the door.

"Come, come gentlemen. This is a Stradivarius on offer!"

"Tarisio doesn't think so." shouted out a voice, rudely.

"Nor do any of us." added another.

In a very few seconds there was a confused babel of voices. Everybody was talking at once. The noise was made worse by the auctioneer banging his wooden hammer on the table. At this point Tarisio caught Pierre's eye and gave a faint nod. Quietly, he slipped out by a side door. His work was done, it was now up to Henri. If he, too, played his part well, they would both have money in their pockets by nightfall. He grinned as he walked towards the rendezvous to wait for Tarisio, Henri and the violin.

Gradually, the auctioneer restored order.

"Gentlemen! Gentlemen! Please!" he called out. "For the last time who will bid me one hundred for the Stradivarius violin?"

The stony silence which followed was suddenly broken by a shout form the doorway.

"One moment, Monsieur. One moment, I beg you."

With the violin case held tightly under his arm, Henri picked his way clumsily between the furniture, a silly grin spread over his face. He passed close to Tarisio without so much as a glance.

"One moment Monsieur." he repeated. "I would make an offer for the fiddle, for it certainly looks better than mine. But first I must see if I have enough money."

Dropping his violin case on a chair beside him, he started to turn out his pockets and count aloud.

"Seventy, eighty, ninety. Ah. One hundred. I bid one hundred Monsieur."

The auctioneer shrugged his shoulders and called out,

"One hundred francs I am bid."

"No, no, Monsieur. Not francs. One hundred centimes." cried Henri in great alarm.

A roar of laughter greeted this and Henri grinned amiably in pretended stupidity.

"The fellow's an idiot." snapped the old gentleman.

"Not such an idiot if he gets a Strad, for a hundred centimes."

"Hmm! You're singularly innocent for a violin dealer. If Tarisio has not bid, the instrument is worthless."

Margaret realised now what Tarisio had done and that his cunning plot had succeeded, and she felt so angry seeing the Professor's violin sell for just a few coppers.

It was now obvious that there were to be no more bids and the sale was closed with the centimes offered by Henri.

"Sold to the gentleman with the fiddle box." came sadly from the auctioneer. With a sigh he handed the violin to his clerk who passed it to Henri in exchange for his handful of coppers.

Margaret winced when she saw how roughly Henri was handling the delicate instrument. She knew just what it must be thinking. The sale was continuing, only she didn't wait to hear any more, but hurried after Henri who was already by the door, hugging both the old fiddle case and the Professor's violin. Once outside in the street she had no difficulty in following him, knowing that he would lead her to Pierre and the rascally violin dealer, who had also left the auction as soon as he had seen that his plan had succeeded. However, she had not bargained for quite such a long walk. Henri set off at a rapid pace, twisting and turning through the narrow streets until at last he stood before the door of a shabby old house on the outskirts of the town. He was about to knock when the door opened and Pierre beckoned him in with a grimy finger.

No sooner was door closed, then Margaret opened it again, to find herself in a dirty little room, which looked as if it had never seen soap and water, dustpan or broom. On the far side was another door which led to a second room, from which came the sound of voices. Creeping softly over to the door, she peeped in. Henri and Pierre were sitting at a table, and between them lay the Professor's violin. Quite near them, was a small stove and on it, bubbling away merrily, was an iron coffee pot. She could smell the coffee, the only pleasant smell in the whole house.

"Well, what do we do with it now?" Pierre was asking.

"Why, take it to Monsieur Tarisio of course." replied Henri. "We shan't get our money otherwise."

Pierre smiled.

"We could sell it to someone else. Another dealer. We might get more money that way."

"Maybe." Henri looked doubtful. "But if we do that, Monsieur Tarisio won't ask us again to help in his little adventures."

Annoyed because he had not thought of this himself, Pierre looked fiercely at the violin and snarled,

"Why anyone makes such a fuss about a fiddle, I can't for the life of me understand. They all look alike to me."

Henri scratched his head, looking puzzled.

"I don't either." Then an idea struck him.

"Perhaps there's money inside."

Pierre looked closely at him. Did Henri know something he didn't? Then he picked it up and peered inside, shaking it vigorously.

"Bah! Nothing." Then he added suspiciously, "You didn't find anything I suppose, on your way here?" He looked so savage, that poor Henri got up in alarm.

"Of course not Pierre. I would have shared it if I had."

Pierre seemed satisfied, for after giving the violin a further shake, he tossed it carelessly back onto the table.

"Alright. Alright. Take the thing into the other room and we'll have some coffee while we decide what to do."

Obediently, Henri carried the violin into the other room where Margaret was standing behind the door listening. He put it in a chair and went back to Pierre. As soon as the door closed she hurried over and kneeling down put her ear to it. As she did this the faint sound of vibrating strings came to her, followed by the tiny voice she now knew so well. It positively quivered with indignation.

"Did you see the way he shook me Margaret? Did you see? The great lout! The ignorant rogues actually thought I was valuable because I had money inside me."

Quickly, Margaret bent down again and picked it up, holding it once more in her arms. The soothing effect of her touch was almost magical. The tiny sound post which had been burning so fiercely that the whole instrument seemed to be surrounded in a halo of pale yellow light, now faded into the familiar soft, warm glow.

"Ah, that's better. It's good to know that there are some people about who know how to handle me properly. Sorry I lost my temper."

"I'll put you back on the chair in case Pierre or Henri come back."

"Yes. They'll be in as soon as they finish their coffee."

"Will they sell you to another dealer, or take you to that horrid Tarisio as they promised?" Margaret asked curiously.

"That's what I wanted to talk to you about. In a few minutes they will carry me off to Tarisio. But there's no need for you to come with me. It's not very interesting."

"Oh. I thought I would be seeing him again." she sounded quite disappointed.

"Oh, you will, you will. But first Tarisio takes me back to Italy, to add me to his collection. I think the best idea would be for you to meet me at his house, or home rather – if you can call it a home." finished the violin doubtfully.

"Why? Isn't it very nice then?"

"No. If anything it's worse than this place. He lives alone in a tiny attic over a cheap restaurant in Milan."

The sound of chairs scraping next door told them that the thieves were preparing to leave for their meeting with the unscrupulous violin dealer.

"As soon as we have left, start counting." whispered the violin.

"Yes, I will." she whispered back. Then, as an afterthought, she added, "Will you be there when I open my eyes?"

"Perhaps not at the exact moment. You can't be certain to the minute when you're time travelling. Don't worry about me though. Just go up the stairs at the side of the restaurant and open the door you will find at the top. That's the door to the attic. By the time you have recovered from your surprise, I shall be with you."

As she moved quietly over to the far corner of the room, the door opened, and Henri came in, closely followed by Pierre. Pierre picked up the violin, tucked it under his arm, then changed his mind and handed it to Henri.

"Here, you carry it, just in case anyone from the sale room sees us."

The next moment she was alone in the dingy little room. With a sigh of relief, she closed her eyes and prepared once more to continue her strange journey. She started to count.

Chapter 11

Tarisio's Attic Home and his Remarkable 'Family'

A very different scene greeted her when she woke this time. She was out of doors and the warm sun no longer shone. Instead, huge great clouds chased swiftly overhead and snow lay deep in narrow cobbled streets. It was winter, and the day was fast fading into evening. In front of her, its creaky old sign swinging noisily in the cold wind and announcing to all who were minded to look, that here was the 'Petit Gamin' – was the restaurant. Pressing her nose against the window, she tried to peer in, but it was impossible to see anything at all.

As she cautiously picked her way over the snow until she came to the door, she was looking around her in wonderment. She certainly was travelling! Different times, different places. First Italy, then France, now Italy again. Milan the violin had said. She opened the door and peeping round could just make out forms of people seated at tables eating and drinking. Several candles flickered unsteadily, in various parts of the room, casting a strange yellow light and queer shadows seemed to dance threateningly in the far corners. She bobbed back quickly and started to close the door as a man with a bald head and wearing a very dirty apron, which may once have been white, came across to the window.

He passed a greasy sleeve over it and the she saw his face close to the glass. She heard him grunt and then turn to his customers and say,

"It's stopped snowing. Maybe there'll be a few more people about now."

"What a horrid place to eat in." Margaret thought to herself. Still, at the moment, she had more important matters to see to. So, walking carefully over the icy surface of the cobbles she went to the other side of the door, and there, exactly as the violin had told her, she found the staircase.

There was no door. Just a flight of rough wooden steps leading up to blackness above. For a moment she hesitated. It really did look very dark, and she wondered how she was going to see the door into the attic. Once she started though, her fears vanished. In fact, as her eyes became used to the dark, she found she could see quite easily. Up and up she climbed, stopping at each turn in the stairs to catch her breath, until at long last, she was at the very top of the house. There in front of her was the door to the attic. It was fastened with a large padlock. Tarisio may have lived in a hovel, but he certainly did not intend any unexpected guests to come visiting!

Margaret looked at the padlock and sighed.

"Oh dear. It looks as though I shall just have to sit on the stairs until someone comes." she said aloud to herself. Then another thought came to her. Of course! The violin had said – 'Just open the door and walk in'.

Getting up from her seat, she cautiously tried the handle of the door. It opened easily, as if there had been no padlock at all.

Softly, she stepped into the tiny attic and closed the door. She was able to see quite clearly, in spite of the fading light, for part of the sloping ceiling was made of glass. It was all very dirty, with here and there a long crack hastily repaired with paper. And she saw cobwebs hanging in the corners, which only added to the woebegone appearance of Tarisio's home. A small table stood in the centre of the room and a chair with a broken back was thrust carelessly under it. On the far side stood a small bed and close at hand a wooden chest. Two candles stood upright on it, in their own grease, with a third on the floor where it must have fallen. Lastly, next to a window looking out onto the snowy street, was an empty fireplace. That, in short, was the entire contents of the little attic, with one important exception.

Violins! Everywhere she looked there were violins. On the walls, hanging from pieces of string from wooden beams which crossed part of the ceiling. On the bed, the table, even the floor. In this tiny room were more fiddles than in the entire workshop of old Stradivarius. But, whereas all the ones there had all looked alike, being made by the same master hand, these were of every kind and colour. Some shone under many coats of deep brown varnish, others were a dull reddish brown or amber. A few were even pale yellow. Most had the usual scroll, but a few were decorated with the carved head of a lion or a bearded man, and one, which was hanging from the ceiling, was inlaid with most beautiful coloured woods. Even its pegs, which were made of rosewood, were inlaid with mother-of-pearl.

As she stood on tiptoe to look at it more closely, another caught her eye. It was hanging with its back to her. Rich brown in colour, the entire back was carved to represent a monk at prayer. The folds of his habit, the rosary in his hand and the staff laying beside him were all perfect. He even had wrinkles on his forehead! Pulling the broken chair out from the table, she climbed on it to look more closely at the two beautiful violins. Then she turned round and whispered,

"Can any of you talk to me?"

The very lightest of murmurs sighed gently through the silence of the little attic, and then was gone... As she touched the carved wood she felt it tremble and she was sure that from various parts of the room she could hear the gentle creak of expanding wood, but there was no reply.

Once again she tried.

"Violins, can't any of you say something?"

This time the murmur came a little louder, and from the darkest corner, from the bed, came the merest suspicion of vibrating strings. But before she could get down from the chair to go over and look, it had stopped.

Disappointed, she stood by the table and started to count the violins, but at one hundred and twenty she gave up. It was now so dark, she couldn't see the ones in the very far corners or on the floor under the bed. Speaking to herself again she said,

"I wonder just how many there are of you here?"

Then quite clearly came the sound she had been waiting for, the soft buzz of strings, followed by a few silvery notes.

"There are two hundred and forty six of us." answered a shy little voice. It came from above her head. So, getting on the chair again, she quickly saw that it was the carved violin which had spoken.

Lifting it down, she sat and placed it on her lap.

"Why won't the others speak to me?" she asked it softly holding the beautiful instrument by the neck and running her fingers over the magnificent carved wood.

"We don't know you." came the equally soft reply.

"Then why did you speak?" persisted Margaret.

"When you touched me I knew at once that you loved violins and I wasn't afraid any more. Besides, I can talk better than any of the others."

"Oh? Why is that?"

"Well, you see, I haven't got much of a singing voice, so I talk more to make up for it."

"How can you say that. Why, you're one of the most beautiful violins in the room."

"Ah. That's the trouble. Beautiful to look at, but all this carving isn't very good for my voice."

"Why not? I don't understand."

"It's this way. The carving makes my back all sorts of different thicknesses, in all the wrong places unfortunately, and of course, that's not good for a violin."

"I suppose that's true. I'd never thought of it before."

"I do wish I had a lovely voice like the others." went on the violin wistfully.

"But surely the violin maker must have known that when he made you."

"I wasn't made by a violin maker."

"Goodness, you do say the strangest things. How could you not be made by a violin maker?"

The violin was growing bolder now, and as it spoke louder, Margaret could indeed hear the roughness in its voice.

"Please tell me about it. Tell me about the person who carved you so wonderfully."

"There's not much to tell." it said. "I was made in a monastery. It took him nearly forty years." Then it added in a very soft voice,

"It was rather wonderful you know, because Brother Ignatius was born blind."

Margaret was silent. Her fingers wandered over the carving, in the darkness of the attic, much the same as those of the monk must have done a century before.

"You must be very proud of him – why even your ribs are carved."

"Yes, even my ribs." replied the violin sadly. "But I do wish I could sing like the others."

"Well, voice or no voice, I think you have a lot to be proud of. I don't suppose there's another like you in the whole world. You must be very rare you know, or else Tarisio wouldn't bother with you."

Before the violin could answer, a tiny voice from above her head joined in.

"I'd like to talk to you too. You see, I can't sing either."

"Good gracious! Not another carved violin?"

"Oh no." said the one of her lap. "That's the one that's all inlaid. But it has the same effect. Beautiful to look at but no voice."

"I remember. The one hanging next to you."

"Yes, that's me." came the pathetic little voice. "But I do have one thing to be proud of. I've got over five hundred separate pieces of wood inlaid in my back – and nearly thirty different kinds of wood."

"But you can't sing!" snapped a spiteful little voice from the far end of the attic.

This seemed to be a signal for all the violins to join in and like a group of naughty children they chanted,

"You can't sing. You can't sing. You can't sing."

"Ssh! Quiet all of you."

There were one or two whispered grumbles, then silence.

"Are there any more of you that can't sing?"

"No, only us." said the violin from the beam where she had replaced it. As Margaret looked round, a sudden thought struck her,

"I shan't have time to talk to all of you before Tarisio comes back, so I think I'd like to have a word with the oldest of you."

"That's me." came eagerly from the foot of the bed.

There was just enough light to see the violin who had spoken. Going over to the bed, she picked it up and carried it over to where she could see it better, under the glass. It was very slim and delicate looking, and dark brown in colour. It had obviously had a very hard life because it had two broken rib corners, and in places the varnish was quite worn away.

"Ah, it's nice to be handled properly, once in a while." it breathed.

"Doesn't Mr. Tarisio handle you carefully then?" Margaret asked.

"Oh yes. I didn't mean that. None of us like him very much, but he does know how to look after us. No. It was all the hundreds of other people who have owned me, before I was recognised as a very valuable instrument. I was made by Nicolo Amati."

"Really?" said Margaret in some awe. "The very first of the great violin makers. I've been longing to meet an Amati violin. Perhaps you can tell me something. Was Stradivarius ever a pupil of his? You see, in my century, some experts' say he was and some disagree. Lots of people say he couldn't possibly have been."

"I can soon put you right on that one." said the Amati, clearing its throat importantly. "Antonius Stradivarius was a pupil of my maker for nearly twelve years. And here's another thing that will interest you. Inside me are two tiny pieces which were the very first carved by the young Stradivarius."

There was a silence for a moment, everyone waiting to hear what was coming next. It went on,

" I well remember the day he came to my master to seek approval of these two corner blocks he had just finished. They were so perfect, that as a reward my master threw his away and used the young apprentice's."

Before Margaret had time to say any more on hearing this interesting piece of information, she heard a few silvery flute notes, then more came urgently from all over the room.

"Somebody is coming up the stairs."

"Somebody is coming!"

She hastily put the Amati back on the bed, then in the gathering gloom she blew a kiss to them all.

"I'll say goodbye then. I don't suppose I shall be able to speak to you again."

"Goodbye, goodbye." chorused the beautiful instruments in every tone of violin voice. Then, as the footsteps came louder, they each settled down once more into silence in their queer hiding places. She tiptoed across the attic and stood in the darkest corner. Suddenly a stealthy whisper broke the silence.

"The chair, the chair!"

"The chair? Where?" she whispered.

"Quickly. Put the chair back as you found it." She just had time to put it back when she heard the sound of a key turning in the huge padlock, and in shuffled Tarisio. In his hand he held a lighted taper and under his arm a violin case. Putting the case on the table, he lit the candles and in a few seconds the flickering light cast an eerie glow over the strange scene. The eccentric violin collector drew his threadbare coat more closely round his thin shoulders and glanced at the empty fireplace.

"Brrr! It's cold tonight. But we can't afford a fire, can we fiddles?" His eyes glanced over his treasures. He touched one of them caressingly with his fingers and set it swinging gently to and fro. Its shadow danced on the wall by her side, and it gave Margaret quite a shock until she realised what it was.

"I've brought another friend to join you, my beauties."

The strange bearded man was talking to his violins as though they were children. She wondered what he would do if they answered back. But except for the heavy breathing of the old man, the attic was quite silent.

He was back at the table now, fumbling with the catches of the violin case. Muttering to himself, he drew the Professor's violin out and with a weird laugh, held it high in the air.

"There, my lovelies, what do you think of this one?" His eyes flashed as he held it aloft and his gloating laugh sent little shudders up and down Margaret's spine. A violin which was hanging quite close to her ear whispered softly,

"It's a Strad."

"I know." she whispered. "It's my Professor's Strad."

"Sssh......Sssshhhh." came from several little voices from nearby.

A moment late she was startled by the noise of a resounding crash as Tarisio swept the empty case off the table. He was now sitting on the broken chair with the violin on the table in front of him. He was crooning softly to himself and running his fingers lightly over the glistening varnish. It was exactly like the pictures she had seen in story books of a miser lovingly counting his gold.

"He's mad." she thought. "Poor old man, his love for violins has driven him crazy."

Suddenly, he wrapped his thin arms around it and hugged it to his meagre chest.

"Ah, my precious. You're much too beautiful to stay here. You shall go to my sister at the farm and keep company with the special ones. They have a nice fire there too, to keep them warm in winter." He stood up then, and waving the violin in the air shouted,

"See, my friends, this one's too good to stay here with you."

An angry murmur swept through them, but only Margaret heard it.

Tarisio stared round at his cherished collection, laughed and then placed the Professor's violin back on the table. Yawning widely, he walked over to the bed, took the two violins off it, and placing them underneath, lay down. He muttered impatiently as it sagged almost to the floor with his weight, just missing the violins. He yawned once more and immediately fell asleep.

"I think he's asleep." said the Amati – the one who was the oldest in the room. Sure enough, at that moment, a loud snore came from the bed and then there was silence once more in the little attic. Luigi Tarisio was sound asleep, dreaming no doubt of all the treasures which surrounded him. Margaret walked over to the table and stared down at 'her' violin.

"I want to talk to the Strad." she explained to the others.

"Which one? Which one?" came a clamour of little voices.

"Oh dear. I'm sorry. I had quite forgotten there would be several of you here."

"Fifteen altogether." called a shrill voice from under the bed.

"Sixteen." put in the Professor's violin sharply. Then under its breath, "And I'm better than the rest of you put together."

Margaret quickly added, (in case any of them heard this last remark)

"It's the new one. On the table." Then turning to it, she went on,

"Now violin, please tell me what I'm going to see next."

The Professor's violin didn't seem to be in a very good temper, and it answered shortly,

"There's not much to see now."

"I'm sure there is. Please tell me. I'm very grateful for all I've seen so far, and for letting me meet all these other violins, but I'm sure there are a lot more things going to happen yet."

"Well." it said, somewhat reluctantly, "Tomorrow Tarisio will take me to Fontinato, to his sister's farm. His most treasured instruments are kept there for safety and I stay there for the next few years. Would you like to go to the farm?"

"Oh yes, I would." cried Margaret excitedly.

"There is one interesting violin that you might see there. Hidden away in an old bureau is a Stradivarius violin which will one day become the most famous violin in the world. I might be able to arrange for you to have a chat with it."

"Not the 'Messiah'?"

"Ah, so you've already heard of it?"

"Everybody who plays the violin has heard of the famous 'Messiah'. Why, in my century I'm part owner of it."

"You are?" said the violin incredulously. "How's that?"

"It's owned by the whole country you see. That's one of the wonderful things about living in my time. Priceless paintings, lovely old buildings, large stretches of the countryside are bought up or given by their owners and looked after and kept for everyone to see and enjoy. The 'Messiah' was given by a well-known firm of London dealers, and is kept in a museum called the 'Ashmolean' in Oxford."

The other violins had all been listening to this and there was an instant buzz of interest. One piped up,

"It must be lovely to be so well thought of." And a sigh came from the wall by the window.

By this time the Professor's violin had lost interest in the subject and talking again.

"Now, here's what you must do." it was saying to Margaret. "I shall be going to the farm tomorrow, but as nothing very much happens for ages, I think you'd better wait a while and come along later."

"You mean I must wait several years?" Margaret looked dismayed.

"No silly. It will be a few years of course, but only a few minutes to you. In fact when we meet again, it will be nearly ten years later. Luigi Tarisio will be dead and another very famous French dealer will visit the farm and buy both me and the 'Messiah'. All of you in this room too."

"I see." Margaret thought hard for a moment. "What year will it be when I see you again?"

The violin was silent, thinking. While he was pondering on this, a voice from the wall butted in,

"It'll be 1854. November 24th."

"All right! All right. I knew that. I would have said it if you'd given me time."

"Thank you." said Margaret to the violin on the wall. Then, turning back to the table she added in some surprise,

"To think, I shall still be more than a hundred and fifty years away from my own time."

"A lot of things can happen in a hundred years." snapped 'her' violin.

"I'm glad they can because then I can look forward to lots more adventures before I have to go home."

The violin was silent once more. Then it said softly to her,

"Well Margaret, I think it's time I said goodbye to you, and you must leave us all. You know what to do by now, don't you?"

"Yes. Goodbye all of you. Goodbye."

Two hundred and forty shrill little voices sadly called their farewells to the visitor from another century, to the accompaniment of several loud snores from the rickety bed. Then everything faded away into silence.

Chapter 12

The Farm at Fontinato

In whatever country we find them farms are usually very much alike. The farm near the village of Fontinato in Italy, was no exception. A large and roomy farmhouse surrounded by outbuildings, cattle stalls and stables, with no claim to tidiness or order. In one corner of the farmyard, deeply imbedded in the frozen mud, stood a rusty plough. Hens scratched diligently for hidden titbits in the frost encrusted grass nearby, and a single fat goose waddled in a patch of unfrozen mud which had been churned up by the hooves of the ten cows which the farm boasted.

This was the picture which Margaret stepped into for her next adventure with the Professor's violin.

Strangely enough, although the winter of 1854 had been one of the coldest in living memory, here in this secluded valley, nestling at the foot of the hills which protected it, the little farm had escaped the worst of the bitter weather. Here, lived Tarisio's sister with her two sons Angelo and Antonio and they managed somehow to make a living out of their few acres of land. Here also, were hidden the few rare violins which the cunning old rogue had placed in the safe keeping of his sister. Because he knew she had not the slightest idea of their value. Nor was she interested. So, he reasoned, she would have nothing to gossip about to her neighbours.

In Milan, where Tarisio had lived in his attic above the restaurant, the weather had been terrible. Horses had been frozen to death in the streets as they worked, rivers and lakes were frozen solid for weeks, and hundreds of poor people froze as they slept. Among those who died, was Luigi Tarisio, for although his pockets were always well lined with money for buying his precious violins he refused to spend money on food or heating for his attic home. One morning, at the height of the cold spell, he did not come down to the restaurant for his usual coffee and roll for breakfast, and when the door to his room was finally broken open, it was to reveal an amazing sight.

The old man's body lay stretched over the table, surrounded on all sides by violins. No comforts, no luxuries of any kind, just violins and more violins. All two hundred or so treasured and beautiful instruments that Margaret had seen some ten years earlier. That's all the room held. Just those and the bed. And the dead body of their owner, who's life had been one long struggle to possess them.

Among the first to learn of Tarisio's death was Monsieur Vuillaume, a well-known violin maker and dealer from Paris. He immediately travelled to Italy to meet Tarisio's sister at the attic where the all the violins were still locked up. She, who hardly ever left the farm, decided to make a holiday of it and took her two sons with her.

When they all met, Monsieur Vuillaume made an offer straight away of 1,000 francs for the lot. Tarisio's sister was delighted and was just going to accept when Angelo, a quick witted young man who realised that the collection must be worth much more if a dealer from Paris was so keen, placed a restraining hand on his mother's arm. Seeming to possess some of his uncle's shrewdness, he started to haggle, and after a long argument, he persuaded the dealer to part with 3,000 francs. Vuillaume was just about to leave, when the old lady said craftily,

"There are more violins!" and coughed apologetically.

"What!" exploded the exasperated dealer.

"Oh yes Monsieur. More violins at the farm. Several that I have been looking after for my poor brother."

Vuillaume now looked at the three Italian peasants who had so neatly beaten him at his own game, then casually asked,

"They are included in the deal of course? I will send for them later."

"Alas, no Monsieur. They are quite separate from these."

"How many are there then?" the dealer finally said wearily.

"Five or maybe six, I think."

For a moment or so, the dealer was undecided, but then to the delight of the three from Fontinato, he agreed to visit the farm the next day and see for himself.

The following day, a few minutes before he arrived, Margaret had found herself sitting before a roaring fire in the farmhouse kitchen which she could see also served as a dairy, since there were pails of milk standing next to a huge stone sink. For the first few minutes after opening her eyes, she couldn't understand where she was. although by this time she was getting used to sudden changes from one country to another, and from summer to winter, all in the space of minutes. Not to mention from one century to another.

The kitchen was quite empty, except for a large sheep dog which lay drowsing on the hearth in front of the fire, right at her feet. Getting up, she carefully stepped over the dog, crossed the room and gazed through one of the windows which overlooked the farmyard. A few hens were picking half-heartedly at the hard ground, and in the distance, walking towards the house, she saw the figures of the two men. She shivered a little at the bleak scene, then went back to her warm seat by the fire.

She could hear voices somewhere, so she decided to investigate, and was just about to get up again and go over to the door, when it flew open with a clatter and the two men came in.

The younger of the two called out,

"Mother, Mother, Monsieur Vuillaume is here."

She looked at the second man. So this was Monsieur Vuillaume, the great French violin dealer. He was tall, very thin, about thirty and wore a short pointed beard, which made him look, Margaret thought, very handsome indeed. The collar of his coat was turned up about his ears when came in, and when he turned it down, she burst out laughing. He was wearing earmuffs! Tiny black bags which fitted snugly over his ears and looked extremely warm and comfortable for the bitter winter weather.

Just then, Madame Lucci, Tarisio's sister, came into the kitchen. She was closely followed by her younger son Antonio. They welcomed the dealer effusively. They had visions of another business deal, in which they had already planned to drive as hard a bargain as possible.

The Frenchman was not in a good humour. He was cold and anxious to get back to his shop. He frowned heavily and waved away the chair which they offered him,

"The violins! The violins! Come. I have little time to spare."

Without a word, Madame Lucci pointed to the three dusty fiddle cases which she had brought down from the loft. He struggled impatiently with the fastenings and first took out a beautiful instrument by Carl Bergonzi. Without comment or change of expression, he opened the second case and drew in his breath sharply as he lifted out the Professor's Stradivarius from the dirty box where it had been ever since Margaret had last seen it. The third was a magnificent violin by Guadagnini, but, although these three were finer than anything else he had previously seen, he was determined not to betray his excitement to the cunning farmers who were watching him closely.

"You like them Monsieur?" asked Angelo anxiously.

"So, so." replied Vuillaume, praying that his trembling hands would not show his delight at such a find. "Are there any more?"

Madame Lucci pointed to a battered desk, which stood under the window. The smile had gone from her face and had been replaced with a frown of disappointment.

"The bottom drawer Monsieur, but it is stuck fast. The violins are jammed so tightly that we were frightened to open it."

Margaret moved over to the window, where she could see the dealer as he struggled with the drawer. As she passed the Professor's violin, a cautious whisper came to her ears.

"Here I am Margaret."

"Ssh! Be quiet!" she bent over it, "Wait till we're alone."

The violin dealer had managed by now to open the drawer about an inch and peeping in could see the cause of the trouble. Two violins were wedged so tightly, it seemed impossible to open it further without damaging them. But what he saw made him redouble his efforts. With mounting excitement, he tugged and strained until inch by inch the stubborn wood gave way and at last the drawer lay open.

There, lay two of the most magnificent violins he had ever seen. One was a perfect example of the work of Joseph Guarnarius. The other, the mighty 'Messiah' Strad.

For a few moments he gazed at them spellbound. Then, tenderly, he lifted them from their crude hiding place. He was overcome with emotion at his find and could no longer hide his real feelings from the Luccis'.

"It is the 'Messiah' Madame – don't you understand? The one your brother was always boasting about, but which everyone doubted existed. At last I know it really does exist, and I ... I have found it."

"Is it a good fiddle?" asked Angelo, gripping his mother's arm to stop her from speaking.

"A good fiddle? A good fiddle? My friends, it's priceless!"

No sooner had he uttered these words then he could have bitten out his tongue. Holding the two violins, he looked at the smiling and triumphant faces of the three. What he saw there made him shrug his shoulders in resignation.

"You will wish to bargain Monsieur?" put in Antonio.

Madame Lucci beamed expectantly. During the next two hours the bargaining went on. First Vuillaume would increase his offer by a few francs, then Angelo would reduce his demands slightly. And so little by little they at last reached a figure at which both sides were satisfied.

By the time it was all over, Margaret felt quite giddy. At last Monsieur Vuillaume took his leave promising to come back the next day to collect his newly acquired treasures.

After some excited conversation about the amazing value of poor Uncle Luigi's silly old violins, Angelo, Antonio and their mother went off up to bed well satisfied with their afternoon's work. The dog too, followed out to some snug corner of its own.

Immediately she was alone, Margaret took all five violins and placed them on the mat in front of the fire, then settled herself down in the comfortable chair and prepared for a long talk with them.

Chapter 13

Margaret meets the 'Messiah' Strad.

Stirring in front of the fire, in the warm, comfortable farm house kitchen, Margaret looked into the glowing embers, hardly able to believe what was happening, then she looked down at the five violins lying at her feet wondering what they would have to say. On the left lay the Professor's Strad Next came the 'Messiah', then the Guarnarius which was slimmer than the others and rather delicate looking, then the Bergonzi and the nearest to the fire was the Guasagnini.

Suddenly it spoke, "I'm too near the fire." it said grumpily. "The heat will spoil my varnish."

"Sorry." replied Margaret, and hastily moved it further away. "Is that better?"

"Yes, thank you."

"How did you know I could talk to you?" she asked curiously.

"Your Strad, told us. It's talked of nothing else ever since it arrived."

"How long have you been here then?"

"About twelve years, and I'm glad I shall be going away at last. Perhaps someone will play me then. I want to sing again."

"So do I."

"Me too." added the others.

Margaret looked at the last one who spoke in a sweet high pitched voice – the Guarnarius.

"How long have you been here?" she asked it.

"Nearly twenty years. And no one has played me in all that time."

"And what about you?" She was now looking down at the 'Messiah'.

It didn't answer, and Margaret looked at the Professor's violin, rather puzzled at its silence.

"What's the matter with it?" she whispered. "Why won't it talk to me?"

"Oh don't bother with it Margaret." said the Guarnarius. "It's only sulking. Strads often do that. Highly temperamental you know."

There was quite a long pause, while Margaret stared again at the fire. Then the deep rich voice of the 'Messiah' suddenly burst out, quite startling her.

"It's not worth me talking. I'm sure I've not got a voice worth listening to."

"Of course you have. You have a lovely voice."

"That's just what I keep telling him." broke in the Professor's violin. "But he won't believe me."

"Oh, but you have, you have. It's the most beautiful violin speaking voice I've ever heard, and I've listened to quite a lot of you now you know."

"Go on, tell her about it." prompted the Professor's violin.

"Here we go again!" groaned the voices of the others.

"Oh boring!" "Heard it all before!"

"Well." said Margaret. "I've not heard it."

"Very well then. I was made in 1716 by Stradivarius, in the same workshop and at the same bench as your friend here."

"Really?"

"It's now, let me see …."

"Eighteen hundred and fifty four." chorused the others.

"Yes. 1854. That makes me about a hundred and thirty years old, and so far nobody has ever played me. So you see, I still don't know for certain if I have a good singing voice or not."

"Start the story at the beginning." put in the Professor's violin encouragingly.

"Well, as I said, I was made in 1716, about twenty years before Stradivarius died, and I can well remember the day too, when my friend here left the shop in such a hurry. In such a peculiar way too. But then you know all about that, don't you?"

"Yes, I was there and saw it all happen."

"I was hanging on the wall above your head, but you didn't notice me."

"I'm sorry." said Margaret.

"Oh, that's alright. I was just another violin in those days. No one but the old violin maker himself knew that I was the most perfect instrument in the shop. Well, anyway when he died, all the violins in the workshop became the property of his son Paolo, who sold most of us. But he never parted with me, because he liked me so much."

"Go on." put in Margaret, enthralled.

"When he died in 1775, I was sold to a famous Italian collector called Cozio de Salubue, and he valued me so much that he locked me away in his collection for nearly fifty years. Later on I fell into the hands of Luigi Tarisio and I've been here on this farm ever since, so perhaps you understand now, why, although I am so beautifully made, nobody knows for sure whether I can sing or not."

"What a strange story." breathed Margaret. "But tell me, why do they call you the 'Messiah'?"

"Ah. Now that's a strange story too." came the deep rich tones of the mighty fiddle. "It happened after I came here. After Tarisio bought me, he liked me so much he couldn't bear to be parted from me. Then, when he started to travel round again looking for more violins, he put me here for safe keeping. Apparently on his travels he used to boast about me to everyone he met until all the dealers pestered him to bring me out for them to see. He never could bring himself to do this, so one day, a wag to whom he was boasting as usual replied,

"Ah, this priceless instrument of yours is like the 'Messiah' it is always coming but never comes."

That's why everyone calls me the 'Messiah'. Or in French – 'Le Messie'."

"What a wonderful story." Margaret sighed happily. "I've learnt so many marvellous things from all of you and when I get back to my own time and get home, I'm going to persuade my parents to take me to the Ashmolean Museum to see you – that's where you're kept now."

There was a moment of silence while Margaret stared into the dying flames of the fire and thought about it all.

"Well now." said the Professor's violin a little impatiently, "Does anyone else know anything about our family?"

"I was once thrown into a duck pond by accident." said the Guasagnini, joining in eagerly.

"Don't be silly! Margaret's not going to be interested in that."

"Well, I was. I got very wet too and I was nearly ruined."

"What about you?" The Professor's violin looked at the Bergonzi, who thus appealed to utter a series of charming little notes.

"I can't add much about violins – though it's very nice to be asked, but I do know something about bows."

"Now that would be interesting." said Margaret. "I've not heard a single thing about violin bows."

"Right. Now, it so happened that where I was made, there was a very clever man who made violin bows, and they were so good they became sought after all over the world." It stopped, then went on, "I was just wondering Margaret, do you know why a violinist uses resin on his bow?"

"Everybody knows that." snapped the Professor's violin, in a scratching tone.

"Of course they do." added the 'Messiah' quietly.

"Well then, what is the reason?" asked the Bergonzi. "Come on I'm waiting."

"To make it play, of course." they all said in one voice.

"To make it play. To make it play." mimicked the Bergonzi. "You don't know, do you?" it went on triumphantly.

"Go on then." said the 'Messiah' sulkily.

"In the first place did you know that the surface of the bow is made up of horse hairs?"

"Yes." came all the voices, including Margaret's.

"But I bet you don't know that for a very special reason, only twelve in every hundred hairs are suitable for bow making."

"No, I didn't." said Margaret.

"If you look at a single hair under a microscope," it went on, "You find there are tiny scales all over the surface. These little scales lie flat, but when resin is rubbed on, it gets under them making them stand up, so that each hair is like a tiny saw."

"Ooooh!" they all said, now quite interested.

"Then when the violinist draws the bow across the strings, the little teeth grip the string and make it vibrate. So you can see how important it is for a bow maker to have the right hairs to make up his bow."

"That's really interesting. Thanks for telling me. That's another thing to take back with me."

"That reminds me. It's nearly time we moved on again Margaret." said the Professor's violin.

"Oh, must we? I'm so enjoying talking to you all. Where do we go this time?"

"We are all going back to France. Paris this time."

"To Monsieur Vuillaume's shop?" asked Margaret.

"Yes, to Vuillaume's shop." it replied. "Where you will see what happens to me next. Of course, it won't be the same Vuillaume you saw today because we're travelling eighty years on. It's his grandson who owns the shop now – and you won't see him because his manager Louis is the one who hands me over this time. You will see the 'Messiah' though, in his special glass case there. Now Margaret, I think you'd better put us all back where you found us, and get ready for your next journey." said the Professor's violin briskly.

One by one, she picked up the beautiful instruments and put them back. Only a few grey ashes were left in the fireplace now, but the light from the rising moon, shining through the latticed window and reflecting on the snow, gave enough light for her to see quite clearly.

Outside in the farmyard, the frost glistened in the moonlight and faintly to her ears came the sound of the horses stamping in their stable. She leaned over the Professor's violin whispered softly,

"Goodnight. I'll see you in Paris."

"In Paris." came softly back.

Then with a contented sigh, she closed her eyes.

Chapter 14

The Last Pieces of the Puzzle Fall into Place

"Lucille, you really must be more careful with your dusting. This bass has not been dusted for weeks!"

The words came vaguely to Margaret's ears, as she struggled hard to remember where she was. Gradually it all came back.

"The violin shop in Paris." she whispered to herself, looking all round.

The person who had spoken was a young man of about twenty eight, and from his appearance Margaret judged him to be a young man of some importance. He was, in fact, the manager of the shop and he was calling to a young lady, who at the moment was admiring her reflection in the shop window. She pouted very prettily, reached under the counter, and produced a duster. Dutifully, she dusted the cello which stood in a corner of the shop by the window.

"You are horrible Louis. You know how I hate dusting."

Louis ignored this remark, and coming from behind the counter, ran his fingers over the glass case which stood in the centre of the shop. He looked at his finger tips and frowned. Lucille laughed cheekily and called across to him,

"Oh don't bother with the old 'Messiah'. It's safe enough under its glass case. Which I quite forgot to dust this morning!" She added with a grin.

Louis shrugged his shoulders hopelessly, but stood by while the beautiful dark haired French girl ran her duster lightly over the glass case.

Margaret moved across the shop and looked down into the case. There, sure enough was the 'Messiah'. It had been cleaned by the expert hand of old Vuillaume himself and was now kept in perfect condition by the present owner, his grandson. The bottom of the case was padded with the softest of red velvet, and now, shining brightly against the soft dullness of its velvet background, it looked almost regal and certainly very comfortable.

Under the watchful eye of Louis, Lucille was now plying her duster with more energy, so Margaret wandered round the shop, looking for the Professor's violin. She couldn't' find it, but she did recognise several instruments that she had met before. The magnificent carved violin which had been made by the blind monk, hanging on the wall next to a fiddle which had the carved head of a lion in place of the usual scroll. The monk's violin quivered ever so slightly as she looked at it and she felt sure it had recognised her. Cautiously she whispered,

"Hello."

"Hello Margaret." it said softly. "It's good to see you again."

Just then, the tinkling of the shop bell made her turn round to see a small boy of about ten carrying a roll of music under his arm.

"Hello Francois." said Louis, smiling down at the boy. "More practice?"

"Yes please Louis, and may I borrow the Stradivarius?"

"Of course Francois. Monsieur Vuillaume has given me instructions that you can use the Strad. as often as you wish, as long as you don't take it from the shop." He opened a large wooden cupboard, took out a violin and handed it to the boy, who took it and clasped it lovingly in his arms.

"Oh, I wish it were mine, Louis. It's the most beautiful violin in the world. One day when I grow up, I'm going to buy it."

Louis nodded understandingly.

"It has the loveliest voice in the world too." said Francois.

"It certainly sings well when you play it." replied Louis kindly, handing him the bow.

"Monsieur Vuillaume is a very kind man, isn't he, Louis?"

"He is, Francois. He believes you have a real talent, and he wants to encourage you in your studies. That's why he lends you the violin and allows you to use the practice room upstairs."

The boy nodded and passed behind the counter on his way upstairs. As he reached the foot of the stairs, he paused and smiled shyly at Lucille, who blew him a kiss from her perch on the top of the ladder, where she sat dusting some violins hanging high on the wall.

Francois blushed and ran quickly up the stairs to hide his confusion. With the silvery laughter ringing in her hears, Margaret stared hard at the door which was now closed behind the boy. She was puzzled. Something about the young Francois reminded her of someone she knew quite well, but no matter how hard she tried, she just couldn't remember who it was.

"Francois is a nice lad." said Lucille.

"Oh, the boy's alright." replied Louis. "But we shan't make much money if all our customers use the practice room free of charge as he does."

"Perhaps he'll buy the Strad. if he likes it enough."

Louis snorted. "Buy the Strad? Don't be ridiculous Lucille. He has no parents and he's as poor as a church mouse. That's partly why Monsieur Vuillaume pays for his lessons as well."

Lucille had now climbed down and put away her duster and was sitting on a high chair in front of a large desk. She was studying an account book which was open in front of her. Suddenly, she looked up and listened.

"Listen Louis, he's playing now. He plays brilliantly for a ten year old."

"Yes, quite as well as some of the older students. Of course he is using one of the finest instruments in the shop, which makes a difference."

Slipping from her chair, Lucille went to the door which led upstairs and opened it. From the room above there floated down the voice of the Professor's violin. Margaret knew it at once. She was just deciding whether to creep past Louis and make her way up the stairs, when Lucille closed the door quickly and called to Louis,

"A customer just coming Louis."

"Good. Get back to your desk and look busy." Then, as he recognised the man who had come in, he added under his breath,

"It doesn't matter. It's only old Signor Valleti."

"Strings I expect." whispered back Lucille.

"Yes, and if I know anything about our old music master, it will take him an hour to decide on exactly what he wants."

His groan of despair was instantly replaced by his very best smile as the old violin teacher shuffled up to the counter, while , in her corner behind a very large ledger which hid her face, Lucille giggled softly as she prepared to watch Louis' tactful handling of the crotchety old Italian.

Margaret, intrigued by the byplay between the two, watched curiously as Louis placed a number of packets containing strings on the counter.

"Strings, Signor Valleti?"

The game was a familiar one to Louis, for game it was. About once a month, the old Italian would call to replenish his stock of violin strings. He would begin by seeming to know what he wanted, gradually forcing Louis to place on the counter, every string in the shop. Then he would consider each one, carefully comparing it to the others. He would run his finger delicately along it, while Louis danced in agony in case he left a small portion of grease on the string, thus ruining it completely. He never did of course, but the possibility always tortured poor Louis. After that he tested each with a gauge taken from his pocket. Finally, when Louis' nerves were in tatters, an argument would start as to which were the better, the French ones, or those made in his beloved Italy. Louis always started out with a firm resolve to be polite and helpful to this most difficult of their customers, but in the end, he always succumbed to the old man's baiting and argued as fiercely as the other. Indeed, on one occasion he had so far forgotten himself as to tip a whole boxful of strings over the old man's head.

Lucille always greatly enjoyed these exchanges, to watch the usually calm and correct Louis wave his arms in the air and contradict a customer was quite a bright spot in her hum-drum day. The strangest thing about these encounters was, that no matter how violently the transaction ended, the old Italian would reappear in a few weeks as if nothing had happened, and the game would start all over again.

Margaret was certainly intrigued by the weird clothes the old fellow wore. He was completely covered from head to foot in a long black cloak which touched the ground as he walked. The thin sallow face which peeped out from under the black hat with the largest brim she had ever seen, reminded her of pictures she had seen of Guy Fawkes. The strange customer and Louis were just getting to the stage where Louis' patience was nearly exhausted, when another customer came into the shop. Lucille slipped off her chair and went to greet the new arrival, politely uttering a,

"Good morning."

The customer, a lady was dressed in the very height of fashion and waved Lucille away murmuring with a smile,

"Thank you my dear, but I'll wait until Louis is free."

Seeing the newcomer out of the corner of his eye, Louis mustered all his self- control and continued to smile until the old man had made his final choice saying,

"I'll take these, but they are sure not to last. The French can't make violin strings."

Shaking with supressed anger, Louis put the strings into a bag and handed them to the old man. Then, after carefully watching the well-dressed lady to make sure she was not looking in their direction, he hissed into the startled face of the old teacher,

"Why don't you go back to Italy, you old nuisance."

After old Signor Valleti had recovered from his surprise, he suddenly broke into a torrent of words in his own language and with a quick movement swept a pile of strings onto the floor. Then, clutching his purchase after throwing his money down and still calling the most awful penalties upon poor Louis' head, he rushed out of the shop.

As the door closed with a loud crash, the violins creaked and quivered on the wall, and Louis mopped his brow with his handkerchief in relief.

"A very strange little man." said the lady with a smile.

"Yes indeed Madame." replied Louis. Then he added, "Madame does not speak Italian?"

"I fear not."

Louis sighed with relief.

"Signor Valleti is a little eccentric Madame, but we're quite used to him. He's no trouble at all really."

"Oh?" came the faintly surprised reply. "Well no matter, it's no concern of mine."

"Madame would like to see some violins?"

"No, not particularly. I've called to hear Mallais play."

Louis looked puzzled.

"I beg your pardon Madame."

"I've called to hear Mallais play the violin."

""Mallais? Mallais? I do not recall the name."

"Yes you do Louis. Francois Mallais. The boy upstairs."

It was Lucille speaking.

"Your pardon Madame. Of course, Francois. I am not familiar with his surname. But I still do not understand. Francois is but a child."

"So I understand from Monsieur Vuillaume. I wish to hear him play."

Still completely at a loss why this obviously wealthy lady should want to hear a mere child at his practice, Louis was about to voice a further protest, when the quicker witted Lucille darted forward and running to the door, flung it open.

"Nothing easier Madame."

The lady smiled her thanks, then turning to Louis asked,

"Is that the boy, Mallais?"

Floating down the stairs came the brilliant staccato notes of a well-known violin sonata.

"Yes Madame, that is Francois. Would you like to go upstairs?"

She was listening intently by now and waved away the well-meant suggestion.

All this time, Margaret could hardly contain her excitement. Of course! At the very first mention of the name 'Mallais', she had realised that the ten year old Francois upstairs was none other than her very own Professor. She also knew with a slight sense of regret that she was now only some sixty years away from her own time.

"No wonder I thought his face looked somehow familiar." she whispered to herself.

Chapter 15

A Very Generous Lady

The violin shop was very quiet as they all listened to the music coming from above. Lucille, with her hand still on the door, stood quietly smiling. Louis with a shrug of his shoulders, resigned himself to waiting on the pleasure of this seemingly very important lady. Margaret, unseen by either, listened entranced to the beautiful voice of the Professor's violin in the capable hands of the young Mallais.

A flurry of swift staccato notes followed by a series of arpeggios in a minor key came to them as they stood there. It all sounded quite perfect to Margaret, but Francois, unaware of his unseen audience, was obviously not satisfied, for he kept repeating the passage again and again. With each repeat, the lady silently nodded her head in approval, until finally, she gestured to Lucille to close the door.

"Your master is quite right Louis. The boy is very promising. Exceptional."

"Perhaps it is not all talent Madame. The boy plays upon a Stradivarius violin. One of the finest we have in stock."

For a moment she did not reply. She appeared to be thinking deeply, but just as Louis was about to add to his remark, she said,

"I understand from your master Louis, that the boy is very poor and possesses no instrument worthy of his talent?"

Louis was still very confused. He could not for the life of him think why this grand lady should be so interested in a young and unknown student, and after his exhausting encounter with Signor Valleti, his wits were not at their sharpest. With a puzzled frown, he started to pick up the strings from the floor and tidy them away.

"I do not know much about the boy Madame, except that he is very poor. He has no parents and lives with an aunt in the poorer quarter of the city. Monsieur permits him to use the practice room here free of charge and allows him to borrow the Stradivarius as often as he needs."

"Does he talk of the violin?"

"Madame, he talks of nothing else." replied Louis dryly. He carefully went on sorting the packets of strings. Then he added,

"I think it's the most important thing in his life, for it's difficult to persuade him to leave it behind when goes home."

The alert Lucille, who had been listening intently to this conversation, now left her seat at the desk and walking to the counter, joined in.

"Madame, Francois is a good lad and one day will be a great violinist. Monsieur Vuillaume has said this and he is one who knows. The boy loves that violin with every fibre of his being. If only it were possible that some kind person would buy it for him ....."

"Lucille!" cried the horrified Louis in shocked surprise. "Apologise at once and return to your desk."

Lucille ignored the sternly frowning Louis and looked pleadingly at the lady. To her delight – and Louis' great surprise, she did not seem in the least bit offended. Instead, a warm smile lit up her face.

"That is exactly what I intend to do." she said, after a short pause.

Louis pulled at his stiff collar with a trembling finger, stared, then managed to gasp unbelievingly,

"You'll buy the Strad. and give it to this unknown boy?"

"Yes." she replied, secretly amused by the shocked expression on his face.

"But Madame," he protested. "It is one of the most expensive instruments in the shop."

Lucille clapped her hands in sheer delight. She had been quick to realise what was in the mind of this unusual customer and she now knew that the violin was good as Francois' own already, no matter what the price was.

"Madame, Madame, thank you. Thank you from the bottom of my heart. You are indeed a generous patron of the arts. Francois will be delirious with joy when he knows ….."

"Be quiet Lucille." snapped Louis. "Madame has not yet made up her mind. How can she when she does not yet know the cost of the instrument."

The whole transaction was fast slipping from his hands into that of Lucille, who with her timely thanks had placed the customer in a position from which there was no going back. However, both Lucille and Louis received a further surprise the very next moment. For it seemed that subject to her approval of Francois' ability, the whole matter had been settled between her and Monsieur Vuillaume several days ago, including the price. This was apparent when she produced a signed receipt authorising Louis to hand over the violin to Francois. Poor Louis gaped at it, then finally managed to gasp,

"Francois will be down in a few minutes Madame. It is the day on which he does his aunt's shopping. You will not doubt wish to give him the violin yourself."

"No, no Louis. You will do that for me. After I have left."

"But Madame, he will wish to thank you." he protested in some surprise.

"No matter. You will please do as I ask. And tell him that I shall watch his progress very carefully. Should he fail to come up to expectations, the violin must be given to some more deserving student."

Then, to soften her harsh words she flashed an elegant smile at Lucille, nodded to Louis and walked calmly out of the shop. It was all done so quickly, that he had no time to reach the door to see his important customer from the premises. It was the first time that he had ever failed to do this in all the years he had been in the shop. Wiping his perspiring brow, he sat down heavily on a nearby chair.

"Two such customers in one day are really too much for any man!"

Lucille laughed.

"Don't worry Louis. You've just sold the most expensive violin in the shop."

"I sold it? Why, the whole thing was cut and dried before she even entered the shop."

"Oh no it wasn't. It depended on whether she liked Francois' playing or not. And she did."

For the first time Louis smiled.

"I'm sorry I was angry with you Lucille, and I'm not so dense that I don't realise that you were more responsible for the sale than I. I would never have dared to suggest it in the way you did."

Lucille's eyes twinkled as she said,

"Well, shall we go up and tell him?"

Margaret now moved quietly across the shop. She had made up her mind to follow them upstairs, so that she could see for herself how the young Francois received the news. Louis, however, was not ready yet. He was still shaken by the events of the afternoon.

"No. We'll wait until the boy comes down." he said at last. Then as he saw the look of disappointment on Lucille's face, he added,

"He'll be down any moment now. He's already stopped playing."

Lucille tip-toed to the door, opened it and listened. Sure enough the practice room above was silent.

"I'll tell you what we'll do." said Louis suddenly. "You go into the back room and make three nice cups of coffee, and when Francois comes down, I'll invite him to join us."

"What a lovely idea." replied Lucille quickly. "We'll tell him over coffee. Oh, I'm just longing to see his face when he knows."

With this, she disappeared through the door at the back of the shop, and a moment later the clatter of cups told Margaret that Lucille was busy preparing the coffee. Louis sighed, looked again at the receipt which he still held in his hand, then busied himself tidying up the counter. A few minutes later, he too passed through the door and was gone from Margaret's view.

Alone in the shop, she stood facing the door to the practice room, listening expectantly for the footsteps on the stairs which would tell her that Francois was returning. For more than anything, she wanted to see again the young Francois Mallais. As she watched the door opened quietly and he appeared. He was holding the Stradivarius violin in his hands, looking at it lovingly. Louis, hearing him, called from the little room behind the shop,

"Francois! Francois! Come and join us in here for coffee before you go."

The boy hesitated a moment, then carefully placing the violin together with the bow on the counter, eagerly made his way to the rear of the shop.

Margaret was about to follow him, when she heard a familiar voice.

"Margaret, Margaret." the Professor's violin called out.

"I'm here." she said softly.

"Don't go with them. I haven't much time so listen to me. We're nearly at the end of our journey, and you know now how I came to be your Professor's. This is the story he said he would tell you sometime. We shall move on sixty years and when we meet again you will be back in your own time. I shall go home with Francois tonight, and you must close your eyes and when I see you again …..well …..you will see."

She was a little disappointed. She would have loved to have seen the reaction of the boy who was to become her Professor, as he was told that the Stradivarius he so yearned for was really going to be his.

Chapter 16

An Unusual Violin Case

"Hello Margaret!"

She blinked her eyes in the strong artificial light, and looked around her, It was quite a small room and contained a dressing table, two chairs, a full length mirror and a large settee which took up the entire length of one wall. On the back of the door hung a man's dressing gown, and a small electric radiator cast a warm glow through the room.

"Hello Margaret!"

Now her eyes were more accustomed to the bright light, she quickly saw that the voice was coming from the settee, where the Professor's violin was resting, propped up against a cushion. She moved over to it and sat down.

"Hello violin. Where are we this time? It looks something like the dressing room where I first met you."

The violin chuckled.

"Nearly right Margaret, but not quit., This is a dressing room, but in Berlin not London. Listen and tell me what you hear."

"I can hear an orchestra playing."

"Open the door and listen. It's the Berlin Philharmonic Orchestra. They're playing an overture. After that it will be my turn."

Margaret closed the door and sat down again.

"Who owns you now?" she asked slowly.

"Iso Meltzac of course, silly. We're nearly home now. In fact it's only three weeks before the time we met in London."

"Oh." she said, even more slowly. "I suppose that means my adventures with you are nearly over." She turned her head and blinked away a tear. The violin was silent for a moment, then it said,

"I'm afraid it does Margaret. This is our last talk together."

"Yes." she replied, trying hard to keep the tears out of her voice. "But it's been a wonderful time. The best time I've ever had in my life and I don't want it to end … ever …..I don't ….. I don't!"

"You wouldn't like to miss your train, would you?"

"No, I suppose not, but …."

"All good things must come to an end you know."

"Yes I know, and it's very silly of me to cry, but I just can't help it."

She put the violin on her lap.

"Where's Mr Meltzac now?"

"Oh, don't worry about him. There's another little room behind this one he's lying down resting. He always does that just before he plays. We've nearly twenty minutes before he'll need me."

"Only twenty minutes!" Her voice sounded very doleful indeed.

"You do sound sad. Never mind now. Come along and tell me how you enjoyed your adventures."

She brightened visibly at the memories. When she had finished speaking, the Professor's violin said,

"Well, you certainly are very enthusiastic. I'm glad it was all such a success. Tell me. You've heard the voices of many of the most famous violins. You've heard them talking and you've heard some of them singing. Which did you think the best? And did you think the 'Messiah's' voice more beautiful than mine?"

This was an extremely awkward question and knowing from experience how sensitive the violin was on the subject of his voice, she wasn't quite sure what to say. After a moment's thought she decided to be quite honest, even at the risk of offending her friend.

"I think the 'Messiah' has the most beautiful voice in the world, though of course, I haven't heard it sing, But ...." Here she paused and looked shyly at the violin.

" Go on. Go on. But what?"

"Well, I still like yours best." she finished.

She knew the violin was pleased, although for a minute or two it didn't say anything. Finally, in a matter of fact voice it said,

"Oh well, don't let's talk about it anymore. Time's getting on and I'm sure there must be more important things to talk about this last time together."

Margaret sighed softly.

"Tell me about the things that are going to happen to you in the future." she said suddenly.

"Ah now, that's something I can't do." it said in some surprise. "I can't see into the future any more than you can."

"Oh." said Margaret blankly.

Then the violin went on,

"It's easy enough for me to take you back into the past because I've already been there and lived through the experiences. But as to what is going to happen in the future, that's quite beyond my powers to see. I may be damaged or broken or even burnt by accident. Or then again, I may even live another five hundred years. Who knows?"

On thinking this over, she realised it had been rather a silly, thing to ask. But she still had another question, so she went on.

"Tell me violin. Am I a very special person, or could you have taken anyone back into the past?"

"Of course I couldn't. You have a very special gift. Don't you remember I told you so when we first met? It was only because you truly love violins that I was able to talk to you at all."

"Yes, I remember now. So many things have happened that I'd forgotten that."

The violin appeared to be thinking deeply, so she waited politely for it to continue.

"Have you ever thought Margaret, that there must be hundreds and hundreds of very fine violinists who, although they love music, just use us violins as a means through which they can express that love. They never think of us as something quite unique. We are you know. For instance, very few people realise that we are one of the few things in your modern world that can't be improved on by science or modern technology. A violin is made today in exactly the same way as it was two hundred years ago. I doubt if you can think of a single thing in your time of which the same could be said. I think that's rather wonderful, don't you?"

Margaret nodded.

"Yes it is. I've always loved violins for that very reason, and one day I'm going to own one like you."

The violin sighed. A fat tinkling sound.

"Wouldn't it be lovely if one day you owned me?"

Margaret's heart began to beat faster at the very thought.

"It would be wonderful, wonderful. We could talk and talk …. and we could go back and find all the little adventures you ever had, and I should never get tired of playing you."

"And I would never get tired of singing for you." the violin put in eagerly.

"But I shall never play well enough to own a violin as wonderful as you." she sighed. "Besides, I should never have enough money to buy you."

"Money would be the least of your worries. You seem to have forgotten that in the first place I was given away by old Stradivarius. Then later, I was given to your Professor, who in turn gave me to some promising young violinist."

"Do you mean, that if I worked really hard and practised and practised every day until I could play really well, the Professor might persuade Mr. Meltzac to give you to me?"

"Perhaps." said the violin cautiously. "But it would depend of course, on just how well you could play. One never knows. Practise is the thing. Even Paganini practised ten hours a day."

"I'll do it." said Margaret determinedly. "I'll start tomorrow, directly I get home from school. I'll practise and practise until the Professor will just have to admit I'm good enough. I'll go on to study properly and I'll play every note a hundred times until I can play perfectly, I'll ...."

"It'll be very hard work." interrupted the violin.

"I don't mind." she replied passionately. "If only I knew there was a tiny chance that Mr. Meltzac would think of me when he's ready to pass you on to someone else."

The violin sighed again.

"It would be lovely, if it really did happen. If you and I could meet again in perhaps ten years' time and then stay together for always."

"I'll promise to work hard, then it will just have to happen."

By now the violin was becoming as enthusiastic as Margaret about their plans for the future, when there was a most unexpected interruption.

"Just a minute. Isn't there a place for me in these plans you're making? Where do I come in?"

It was the sweet little voice of another violin.

"Whoever is that?" Margaret turned round in surprise, looking all round, for she hadn't noticed a second violin anywhere since she'd been in the dressing room.

"Oh, that's the Amati. It's in our case over there behind the curtain."

Margaret put the Professor's violin down on the settee again, crossed the room and pulled back the curtain. There, she found the most beautiful red leather case. Laying it carefully on the floor, she undid the clasps and opened it. It was much larger than most cases and quite a different shape. To her surprise she saw that it was made to hold two violins and four bows. One of the plush beds was empty. She turned to the Strad. and said,

"So this is where you live when Mr. Meltzac isn't playing you?"

"Yes."

"It's certainly a most comfortable home."

She looked at the fiddle lying in the second half of the case, but before she had time to say anything, is said shyly,

"I should like to talk to you too please."

"Of course you shall." Margaret replied, lifting the delicate instrument from its resting place.

She carried it across to the settee where she placed it by the side of the Stradivarius.

"I don't know why you can't mind your own business." said the Professor's violin crossly."

"But it is my business." protested the Amati. "We're both owned by Mr. Meltzac, and anything that concerns you, concerns me. Besides, we both live together in the same case. Surely that entitles me to know what's going on."

"Well, it doesn't, so I'll thank you to keep out of it."

"Now, come along you two." put in Margaret, "I'm sure neither of you meant to be rude, but it's not very good manners to argue about such a silly thing in front of a guest."

"Sorry Margaret." said 'her' violin.

"I'm sorry too." added the silvery voice of the Amati.

She looked down at the two instruments, smiled and said softly,

"Alright. Now, tell me why does Mr. Meltzac carry both of you about on his travels?"

"Oh, that's easy enough to answer." said the Amati, eager now to join in the conversation. "The Stradivarius and I have quite different voices."

"Yes thank goodness, I can sing." said the Professor's violin rudely.

The Amati ignored the remark, so Margaret stayed silent, waiting for it to continue.

"The Stradivarius has a remarkable voice. Very clear and loud, with great carrying power and Mr. Meltzac uses it when he is playing in a large concert hall like this one, with an orchestra."

"Very nice of you to say so." said the Strad. politely. Then it added as an afterthought, "Sorry I was rude to you just now."

"Now my voice." went on the other, "although very sweet and clear, has very little carrying power, so Mr Meltzac only uses me when he is playing in a private house or small hall, and accompanied by a piano. If you look at me closely, you will see that I am much slimmer than our friend here, and more finely built."

"That's not true!" interrupted the Professor's violin quickly. "You know very well there is only a sixteenth of an inch difference between us. Nothing to boast of anyway."

Margaret highly amused by the rivalry between them, stayed silent, waiting to hear what the Amati had to say to this.

"I'm not boasting, and as you very well know, one sixteenth of an inch in a violin is quite a lot of difference. Besides I'm nearly sixty years older than you."

Margaret thought it was time she joined in before another argument started.

"I've never heard you sing, of course, but you must have a lovely voice or else Mr. Meltzac wouldn't own you."

Sounds of movement were coming from the other room, so all three remained silent, listening.

"Is that Mr. Meltzac getting ready?"

"I expect so." replied the Strad. "But no need to worry, he won't be ready for me yet."

"Shall I put the Amati away just in case he comes in unexpectedly?"

"Good idea. He would be surprised if he found us both here on the settee."

"You want to get rid of me." accused the Amati sulkily.

"Yes!" snapped back the Strad.

"I think I had better put you back now, Mr. Meltzac might think I'd been meddling with his violins and I wouldn't like that." Margaret bent down to pick it up.

"Oh, I don't think he'd mind if he knew it was you Margaret." put in the Strad.

"Alright then. Put me back." said the Amati in a resigned voice. Then went on,

"I shouldn't like you to get into trouble on my account."

"Don't be silly." snapped the Strad. "Nobody can see her, so nobody knows she's here."

"Oh, I forgot that."

Gently, Margaret carried the Amati back to its case. As she laid it down, it let out a sudden wail of distress. She was nearly startled out of her wits.

"O, oh, you've put me back in the wrong bed."

Another cry came from behind her. This time of rage.

"Margaret. Take it out of my bed at once. At once, I say, I am most particular about my bed. The Amati is a different shape from me, and now I shall be most uncomfortable. In fact, I doubt if I shall ever be comfortable again."

Margaret smiled to herself as she put the violin back into its own part of the case, apologising softly as she did so. Then she closed the lid and put it back exactly as she had found it. She came back to the settee, to find the Professor's violin still grumbling to itself.

"I'm sure I shall never be comfortable again."

"Don't be silly. The Amati was only in your bed for a few seconds. It can't possibly make any difference."

"You don't understand Margaret. The Amati is smaller and lighter than me and its edges will disturb the plush lining. Then later on when I'm put to bed, little pieces of the plush will stick up in my back, and believe me, that's very uncomfortable."

"Look, I made a mistake and I said I'm sorry. It's no good going on about it."

The violin was quiet for a moment or two, then in a different tone said,

"Time's nearly up Margaret. We shall have to say goodbye in a very few minutes."

She sat down beside the violin once again and gently stroked the glistening neck and scroll.

"I don't want to say goodbye." she whispered brokenly.

She had been dreading this moment ever since the violin had told her that this was their last talk together. She hastily turned her head away as a tear trickled down her cheek. She was groping for her handkerchief when it happened. The door opened, and the tall figure of Iso Meltzac walked in. From the hall beyond there was the sound of applause. The orchestra had finished playing and the violinist was due to go on.

She had no time to stand up. No time to think even, for the great Meltzac instantly picked up the violin and was striding towards the door in the twinkling of an eye.

"Goodbye violin. Goodbye." she called out. Frantically she tried to brush away the tears so that she could catch a last glimpse, but the door was already closing as it's sweet little voice, which she had come to love so well, called out to her in reply,

"Goodbye Margaret. Goodbye. See you in London."

Tearfully, she went to the curtains and pulled it aside looking once more at the beautiful red leather case. Going down on one knee, she rested her face against it and whispered,

"Goodbye Amati."

The very faintest of whispered replies came to her ears. Then, crying as though her heart would break, she came back to the settee, sat down and closing her eyes began the last of the magic counts. One...two...three...four....

Chapter 17

Back Home

Slowly and reluctantly, between her sobs, Margaret carried on the count which would take her back to the dressing room in London. This time the sensations were quite different. She began to feel very drowsy, and before she had reached halfway, she was so weary that she knew that she would soon be fast asleep. Her last conscious thought was vaguely wondering what would happen if she fell asleep before she reached a hundred.

Back in London, in the dressing room behind the stage, Professor Mallais and Iso Meltzac were still deep in conversation.

"Paris, Vienna, Rome, Berlin and now London. I've seen them all, but in London the warmth of my welcome has exceeded all the others."

Meltzac was speaking and his eyes were sparkling with enthusiasm and pleasure as he recounted his travels to the old Professor.

"Ah Iso my boy, it was ever the same, even in my day. London appreciates the true artist. The English have always been lovers of fine music and musicians. No matter from which far country they come, a welcome is always assured in England."

Meltzac was about to agree with the Professor when his eye fell on Margaret still asleep in her chair.

"Professor! Professor! Both of us have completely forgotten your little friend. See, she is sound asleep with the Strad. in her arms. The poor child must have been bored by our selfish chattering." He glanced at his watch.

"Do you realise we've talking for nearly an hour. NO wonder the poor girl fell asleep."

The Professor peered short-sightedly at the corner of the room where Margaret sat.

"Dear me. Dear me. I'd quite forgotten her in the excitement of seeing you again."

The two men moved over to her.

"Why, she's crying." said the violinist suddenly.

"She must be crying in her sleep. Here, take the fiddle from her arms before it falls. I think Iso it's time to wake her."

"We really must apologise to her for our rudeness." said Meltzac as he gently took the violin from her encircling arms. The Professor put his hand on her shoulder.

"Wake up Margaret! Wake up child! It's time to go home."

Two large tears rolled swiftly down her cheeks as the Professor shook her.

"Wake up." he repeated.

Very slowing her eyes opened. For a long time they seemed to gaze blankly into space.

"My goodness. She has been sleeping soundly Professor. We ought to be thoroughly ashamed of ourselves."

The old music master nodded and smiled sympathetically at his young pupil.

Suddenly a look of panic spread over her face. She struggled to sit up in her chair, and the poor old Professor grew quite alarmed.

"The violin! The violin! Oh, what's happened to it?"

"It's alright my dear. Don't worry. I took it from your arms while you slept." said Meltzac soothingly

She looked vaguely at the two faces smiling down at her.

"You've been asleep."

"No! No! I've been away! I'm back now, but I've been away with the violin."

"She's been dreaming," said Meltzac, smiling at the Professor, as the old man looked at his pupil in astonishment,

"Are you feeling quite well my dear?"

"Yes thank you Professor. But I really have been away with the violin. I saw it being made by old Stradivarius in Cremona, and I heard poor Paganini playing on it just before he died. And I saw the wicked Tarisio too ....." Then she saw the look of blank astonishment on the Professor's face, so she finished lamely,

"Perhaps I was dreaming after all."

"Of course you were my dear. Of course you were."

The old Professor beamed at her, pleased that she was looking herself again. But a strange look had come onto the face of Iso

Meltzac. He stood with the violin under his arm, thoughtfully stroking his chin with his long supple fingers.

"Did you say Tarisio, Margaret?"

"Yes, that's right, Tarisio."

"Do you remember his first name?"

"Of course, it was Luigi."

The Professor looked at his friend with a puzzled expression. He was about to speak when the violinist motioned him to be silent.

"And you did say, didn't you that Paganini played on the violin. This violin?" He held it out for her to see.

"Yes I did. He played on it when he was ill in bed. It was in Nice, in the villa belonging to his friend ……"

"The Count de Cesole?" interrupted Meltzac excitedly.

"That's right. But how did you know?"

The Professor, by now completely bewildered by this conversation, looked appealingly at Meltzac for some explanation.

"Well, that's just about the strangest thing I've ever heard." said the violinist.

Margaret was wide awake now and she listened intently as the violinist turned to the old Professor.

"I haven't had a chance to tell you yet, but a year or so ago, I started to try and trace the history of our violin. I wasn't very successful. Except that I did find out that it was once owned by the Count de Cesole, a wealthy Italian nobleman. If this is true, it is quite possible that it was played on by the great Paganini, for they were great friends. Paganini in fact died at the home of the Count in Nice, exactly as Margaret described."

The Professor opened and shut his mouth several times, but was unable to say a word. He looked at Meltzac then at Margaret, finally shaking his head and waving his hands about helplessly, as his old friend went on.

"I managed to trace it back to the time Vuillaume owned it, but before that there is nothing definite to go on. But this proves it. Our violin, Professor, was once used by Paganini, the greatest violinist of all time."

The Professor had recovered a little by now.

"I still fail to see how Margaret's dream can prove anything, my dear Iso."

"Oh, but it does." burst in Margaret, "And it wasn't a dream. I actually saw him playing it. I really did – and I can tell you exactly what happened to it from the time it was made, right up to when you played in Berlin three weeks ago."

She then recounted her adventures, while the two men stood open mouthed in astonishment. Lastly she described how she had carelessly put the Amati back in the wrong side of the case after talking to it. Meltzac nodding, asked her to describe it in detail. Quite easily she did so, and she added that she had never seen one like it before. She also mentioned how she had admired the beautiful red leather and the blue plush lining. Without a word, the violinist left the room and returned minutes later carrying the very case that Margaret had seen. He placed it on the table before the amazed Professor.

"It was made for me in Vienna Professor. It has been kept locked in the Manager's office."

As he spoke, he opened it and brought out the Amati violin.

"There's your proof Professor."

The poor bewildered Professor feebly nodded his head,

"But violins don't talk." he protested half-heartedly.

"Perhaps they do. To some people." said Meltzac, and he smiled understandingly at Margaret.

Made in United States
Cleveland, OH
20 April 2025